MW01357093

Kissing the Blarney Stone

L. Beth Campbell

KISSING THE BLARNEY STONE

L. BETH CAMPBELL

ISBN-13: 978-1-960639-07-3

Case Cover Art and Layout by L. Beth Campbell

Jacket Art by Alexia Roberts Anderson

lbethcampbell.com

To Aunt Jean, even though you're on the other side of eternity, your words and prayers continue to have an impact

PROLOGUE

Nothing could have prepared me for the lasting effects of jet lag. I had scoured multiple articles with tips on how to reduce the grogginess, including making gradual changes to my sleeping schedule to accommodate the time change that comes with a transatlantic flight. One would think that sleeping as much as possible on the plane would guarantee enough energy upon landing, but about two hours before we arrived at the destination, I had woken up without being able to get more rest. My saving grace was the pack of dark chocolate-covered espresso beans that Kendrick surprised me with when he offered to help me pack for this trip. Jet lag was a small price to pay to see the beauty that surrounded me.

Ireland wasn't my first choice as the destination for this family vacation. My older sister, whose boyfriend comes from Irish descent, had been studying Irish history and culture and was the first to voice her opinion when our parents asked for our input. My younger brother graduated from high school a few weeks ago and had suggested Rio de

Janeiro or somewhere in the Amazon. On the other hand, I had been begging for a trip to Italy for years. Usually, I was told a vacation like that for all five of us wasn't in the budget. This time though, I was outvoted. I know it wasn't on purpose, but I couldn't deny that I hadn't seen this happen in other situations in my family. It came with the territory of being the middle child. Again though, there wasn't much I could complain about since most people my age didn't have parents who would bring them along on free vacations. My friends in their mid-twenties were all spending their money and vacation time on domestic road trips within their limited budgets.

Today might have been the first day I felt adjusted to the six-hour time jump between home and here. Ironically, today was also our last full day in Ireland before our flight back to the United States. Per my mother's request, we're now outside Cork to spend what time we have left at the Blarney Castle and Gardens, our last adventure before the train ride back to Dublin.

By the time we arrived at the entrance to the grounds, my sister had already memorized the map and planned which routes to take to make the most of our few hours here. Meanwhile, I was trying to make sense of why there's a Blarney Castle different from the Blarney House. It seemed that the appeal of the castle was more how old it was for something that's still partially standing—especially old to American tourists living in a country that's only about 250 years old. "The original Blarney Castle is thought to have been built before 1200," my sister read from her guidebook before securing it in her backpack.

The crunch of gravel underneath our feet combined with the smell of recent rain invigorated my senses. As I had promised to Kendrick, I stopped to take photos every few yards or so, increasing my pace to keep up with my sister after I'd captured the image on my phone. Every night when I had connected to the hotel's wifi, I sent him a few highlights from our excursions of the day. It's not nearly as fun as it would have been to experience all this with my best friend, but it's better than the process was during the days of developed film and disposable cameras. Thanks to advances in technology, I could FaceTime with him or type out a novel-length text to give a summary of the day's activities.

"Keep up, slowpoke," my sister joked as she decelerated her pace. Hours from now, she would be begging me to share these very photos that delayed her plans to walk all the trails on the grounds. That's the biggest difference between our personalities though. Kathleen traveled through life at 100 miles per hour in an attempt to experience as much as possible in little time while I preferred to take the time to be intentional and live in the present. To this day, I was still uncertain how our parents could have biologically produced two daughters who were so very opposite.

"Why exactly did you want to start on the forest trail route rather than go to the castle first?" I asked her out of curiosity. To me, it would make the most sense to go straight to the castle first and then use the remainder of our time to walk the various other routes and attractions that this estate had to offer.

"You'll see," she responded as if she were keeping a secret to herself, though I couldn't imagine anything here that could warrant that type of reaction. Supposedly, these gardens were said to contain a level of enchantment, particularly the section known as the Fairy Glade. The Seven Sisters resembled by the standing stones were just one of the many legends tied to this region of Ireland. It seemed strange to me that they would purposely keep a section named the Poison Garden with warning signs posted. Surely the occasional tourist ignored the strong suggestions and decided to touch one of the toxic plants. Those were the type of people who had to learn lessons the hard way.

"The Wishing Steps," I read from the sign, almost running into Kathleen who had stopped before the first step.

As if she had memorized the line from her guidebook, she stated, "You're supposed to close your eyes and think of a wish while walking down and back up the steps. But you can't think of anything else other than that one wish. Then, your wish will come true within a year. I have a suspicion of what you'll wish for though."

"What is that supposed to mean?" I asked, unsure if I should be offended by her statement.

"Ari," she started with her nickname for me, "I'd be surprised if you wished for anything other than for Kendrick to finally see you as more than a friend. You're not exactly discreet when it comes to the crush you've had on him since high school."

Embarrassed, I tried to cover the truth by saying, "There are more important things in my life to wish for than something I could change if I wanted to." Like a raise, for one. Even a new chair for my desk would make work slightly more pleasant. Although those were both things I could do something about if I were willing to. As much as I wanted to deny it though, Kendrick was the only thing I could think about as I cautiously climbed up and down the steps with my eyes shut. Kendrick's dark brown hair that curled when he went too long without a haircut. The way his cerulean eyes sparkled when he teased me about how color-coordinated my office supplies were. How he always brought an extra cookie for me when we ate lunch together in the break room at work. It was difficult not to want someone whom I'd thought about every day for years.

Once I was finished with the ritual, I waited as my sister performed the same, a smile playing on her lips. She made it look effortless while it had seemed daunting to me to walk up and down stairs with my eyes shut.

"Okay, now we can go to the lake and then to the castle last," she said once her eyes were open again. "I want to make sure that we get to see the lake, so I think it's best if we leave the line for kissing the stone until closer to the end." I didn't question why people would stand in line to kiss an Irish stone, knowing that it would only open the floodgates of information she memorized on the train ride from Dublin to Cork.

The Irish countryside was a depth of green that rivaled that of rainy springtime in Missouri, yet here, it was early summer. I imagined that a leprechaun would be camouflaged well among the emerald countryside, hiding as a rare type of fairy in the foliage.

"So, is this Blarney Lake?" I asked cheekily as we approached the eerily calm body of water.

"Blarney Lough, to be more exact," she corrected. "Supposedly this lough was once thought to have an abundance of leeches." I shivered at the idea of an animal sinking its teeth into my skin to suck my blood. "Calm down, they never found evidence of medicinal leeches in the wild. Enough people frequent here that it would be common knowledge if leeches were lurking around. It's about as unfounded as the legend of the treasure that was thought to be at the bottom of the lough."

"Not that the two are related," I mused out loud, "but I'm not sure if leeches are an effective way to guard an underwater treasure. As gross as they are, they don't kill their prey fast enough." The plants in the poison garden might have been more efficient for that type of job, but then the wildflowers wouldn't be nearly as enjoyable. I attempted different angles to take photos of the landscape with the sun filtering through the trees.

"Sullivan would love all this," she said, quietly enough that she might have meant it for herself. I had never known what to say or how to react when she brought up the topic of her boyfriend, so I defaulted to my usual response of pretending that I didn't hear her comment.

We took a full lap around the lake before heading back toward the castle area on the other side of the grounds. After passing the private walled kitchen garden, Kathleen led us from the lake walk path to the woodland walk toward the Blarney House. The towering mansion better fit what I'd imagine a castle to be, but my childhood was strongly influenced by Disney princess movies. The architectural style was like that of smaller castles in Scotland, though this was an island away. When I looked carefully, I could see shifting shadows through the open windows of the house. "Does someone actually live here?" I wondered aloud to my sister.

"Yes, Sir Charles Colthurst," she responded nonchalantly.

"I'm not sure what's stranger," I said, "seeing people move inside a house at a popular tourist attraction or that he has to deal with tourists ogling at his house consistently. I would hate the lack of privacy that comes with an infamous estate." She shook her head with amusement before persisting that we continue on the path back to the castle.

Centuries ago, Blarney Castle must have seemed grand. Any structures built without the modern technology and construction equipment that we have now would have taken years to build. Like many other castles and fortifications in Europe, the castle that remained likely wasn't the original one built, though this one had been here since the 1400s. Or maybe that was just the tower. While my sister was a helpful source of information, she was far from the level of a professional tour guide. One day, when I had the money to pay for my own vacations, I'd pay the extra fee to have a tour guide who could give me accurate facts about the attractions.

Modern-day buildings weren't built to withstand centuries the way this castle was. The most obvious evidence of aging was in the green that grew along the cracks and crevices, combinations of what must be vines and mildew that wouldn't pass current health standards for living quarters. The lack of an HVAC system was clear by the fireplaces large enough for humans to comfortably stand in, purposely built opposite the areas that would be warmed by the sun. They may not have had the conveniences that we took for granted now, but they were clever enough to plan and work with what they had.

My sister, ever the adventurer, climbed into the abandoned fireplace, not caring what spiders may have taken up residence there. It made sense that this would be the Family Room, as stated by the signs. I tried to imagine a medieval family situated around cooking beef and spending quality time together. Vegans and vegetarians were likely unheard of in those days. Another advantage of our era compared to then was that with the way we bought our raw meat, we could disassociate it from the animal that was killed to provide that meat.

In the castle interior, a set of wooden stairs ascended toward the location of the infamous stone. Another set of stone stairs through a narrow and low corridor later, and we were standing in a line. Unlike the lines at most amusement parks, this one came with a nice view of the countryside from a higher perspective.

I couldn't quite decipher the expression on my sister's face as she chose her words carefully. "Ariella, this is a once-in-a-lifetime opportunity. Legend or not, you should do it just to say you did. Maybe you'll tell your kids about it one day, and they'll want to come here to experience it for themselves."

While there were several versions to the story, the one consensus of the legend seemed to be that anyone who kissed the Blarney Stone would gain the Gift of Eloquence and the Gift of Gab, two things which I did not naturally possess. Kathleen did not need those things since she got the fair share of it at birth. Powers or not, I wanted to have at least one good story to take back home with me, something that would impress Kendrick and our roommates. The idea of lying down and leaning backward over the large crack of open air was unnerving, but for once, I wanted—needed—to be brave.

"I'll do it if you go first," I consented to her. "And I want you to record it in case no one believes me when I tell them." A victorious smile stretched across her face.

Once we were close to the front of the line, I watched the others in front of us to mentally prepare myself. Lie down on my back. Hold onto the two poles. Don't freak out when the worker helps to keep me from falling through the gap between the ground and the wall. Lean backward to kiss the rock. Easy enough. The line moved faster than I would have anticipated until Kathleen was the one hovering over the edge. I was ready and not ready as I mimicked the same motions I'd witnessed dozens of times. Nothing extraordinarily special. No tingling feelings of magic or gained superpowers. Only the adrenaline from the split second that I looked down in midair. I kissed the Blarney Stone.

CHAPTER ONE

Kendrick had offered to pick me up from the airport, but I had insisted that I would be fine riding back to my sister's apartment with her boyfriend and taking the streetcar back to my apartment from there. As much as I hated the idea of his going on a date on a Friday night, I would hate myself more if an unnecessary drive up to the airport were the reason he canceled the aforementioned date. He hasn't gone out on dates much since his break-up with his college girlfriend Sarah, and even if he wasn't on a date with me, I wanted him to be happy. I now regretted that decision.

Sullivan was nice enough, at least when I was around. He lifted both my and my sister's suitcases into the trunk of his SUV without a complaint. As every boyfriend should, he hugged Kathleen and showered her with comments about how much he missed her while we were away. Everything he said and did was a little too perfect and over-the-top, but I'd always had a nagging feeling that there was something he was hiding.

"So, Ariella," he began in an attempt to include me in their conversation, "what did you think of the land of my forefathers?" Sullivan O'Hare might have been of Irish descent, but his family has lived on this side of the globe for a century now.

Before I could think twice, the words spilled from my mouth, "If it weren't for your red hair and complexion, I'm not sure if a true Irishman would recognize you as one of them." Had I just said that out loud? With a peek at one of the rearview mirrors, the look of shock on my sister's face confirmed that those hadn't been mere thoughts running through my mind.

Instead of taking it as an insult, Sullivan laughed and replied, "I've heard the Irish accent enough times to know that you're probably right with that one. Not to mention that I don't even like Irish cream." He might have let my comment slide, but the atmosphere for the remainder of the drive had shifted. My sister's tone was more tense anytime she directed a statement or comment in my direction. I did my best to hide my embarrassment for letting something like that slip. Typically, my reaction was to bite my tongue in hopes of avoiding any and all conflicts. Speaking my mind was reserved for situations in which there were no other options. Besides, my opinion wasn't necessary.

Rather than suffer through more uncomfortable conversations in which I was the third wheel, I put in my earbuds and turned on some music. My phone was still syncing and downloading any missed texts and calls from the hours we spent in the air, and I preferred to catch up now so I could crawl into bed as soon as humanly possible. A few notifications regarding work emails popped up, but none of them were urgent enough to warrant a response before my return to the office on Monday. All that remained were two texts, one from Kendrick and one from my roommate Reagan.

KENDRICK

Want me to come over tomorrow to help you unpack? I know how much you love doing that

REAGAN

I took out the trash and unloaded the dishwasher before leaving for work, so it should all be clean and organized when you get back. I'll be home around 8:30

Reagan's message didn't need a response since she would be home approximately half an hour after Sullivan dropped me off. I could ignore Kendrick's text, but if I ignored him, he would use the spare key I gave him to invite himself over. At least, that was what had happened the last time I didn't respond to his question about hanging out. He was so infuriatingly confident that he assumed the lack of an answer meant yes rather than the other way around. Then he would refuse to admit that he hated to be ignored and claim it was an emergency since I usually responded promptly. Before I could type up a reply that would ensure he took the hint, another message from Kendrick popped up.

KENDRICK

A couple of the guys invited me to play football tomorrow, so unless you absolutely need me (begging possibly required), I'm rescinding my previous offer

Wow, okay. I missed you too. Go ahead and do something fun with the guys. I need to try to get my sleeping schedule back in sync anyway. Wait, aren't you supposed to be out on a date right about now?

She canceled on me at the last minute. Some excuse about her dog being sick and needing to go to the emergency vet. I wasn't that excited about it anyway. Now it means I can help my mom with something she's been pestering me about all week

There was no point in pretending not to be elated at his lack of enthusiasm about this girl. I was well-versed in the art of portraying neutral expressions about issues, despite the strong opinions that I bottled up inside. A few weeks ago when Kendrick had informed me about his joining a dating app, I asked questions to disguise my disappointment. Tonight would have been the first date he's tried going on since we had that conversation. Was my best friend a picky dater, and I was just now noticing it?

You're telling me that Mystery Girl doesn't live up to your high standards?

KENDRICK

We hadn't even been out on one date together, and she started calling me Kenny. You know how much I hate that nickname or anytime someone starts using a nickname without first asking the person. If I wanted to be called Kenny, I would introduce myself as such

It wasn't an exaggeration; he did have a pet peeve about nicknames. I'd never minded the nickname Ari, but in all the years of our friendship, he had never called me that.

Kendrick's mom was the same way about names, always insisting on calling her children by their legal first name and encouraging others to do the same. I could picture her having done that from the time they were born, possibly even using a baby voice with the adult names.

> Did you attempt to correct her, or was it an automatic strike against her chances?

KENDRICK

> Oh, I told her multiple times that I don't like Kenny or Ken as nicknames. I'm relieved I don't have to spend a perfectly good Friday night repeating myself over and over again about that

Comments like that turned me off from considering online dating and dating apps because this girl was one of the better options he had come across. No need to take that bullet myself when I could live vicariously through Kendrick's horrible experiences. Before I could think of how I wanted to respond, Sullivan parked his SUV at my apartment building despite my arguments that I could have taken the streetcar the short distance from my sister's building.

"If it were just you on a normal day, I wouldn't have much problem with that, but you have a carry-on and a suitcase," he pointed out as he pulled my suitcase out of his trunk for me. "Your parents would never forgive me if I let you do that. It's not an inconvenience to drop you off at your building." I glanced at the forty-five pounds on wheels that I'd dragged through multiple airports, grateful that he had ignored my original request. Flying across the ocean had sapped what little energy I had left after all the days of sightseeing.

I still remembered the first time I walked into the One Light Luxury Apartments building in the Power and Light district with Kendrick and Reagan. Reagan had been my college roommate and an obvious choice for a roommate after graduation since we had already learned how to live with each other. Her staying in Kansas City was one less problem to solve when it came to making steps toward a full-adult life. Kendrick's cousin Mikey had planned on being his roommate and had put full trust in Kendrick's (mainly my) ability to pick somewhere nice with a good location.

While the price of rent was the priority factor, we also had to consider proximity to public transportation as well as the availability of two separate two-bedroom apartments. Kendrick and I had made a promise that during this apartment-living phase of our lives, we would live in the same building. Reagan and I let the boys take the apartment with the balcony, and we chose the one with more square footage. If the skyline views weren't enough to convince us, the free Google Fiber Wi-Fi solidified the decision. Since then, Kendrick and Mikey had upgraded to a penthouse with a balcony, my favorite spot to read.

As much as I enjoyed the greenery that Ireland had to offer, there was something comforting about walking into my own space of white walls and concrete ceilings. Through the large living room windows, I could see the lively downtown life, magnified by the fact that it was a Friday night in the glow of summer. On any other night, I would have asked Kendrick if I could hang out on his balcony, but many other things were vying for my attention. Unpack, laundry, shower, and bed, in that order.

I unzipped my suitcase and started sorting my dirty laundry into piles by load type, fully utilizing my laundry sorter. When I opened the washing machine, the faint smell of mildew wafted into the air; the source was a load of towels that had likely been sitting for over a day or two—Reagan. Annoyed, I threw in a cup of white vinegar and started the washer on hot in an attempt to get the smell out of my roommate's towels. If that didn't work, I would let her deal with the consequences since I had enough of my own laundry to take care of before work on Monday.

On the other hand, my shower had been cleaned by that same roommate while I was an ocean away, one less thing for me to put off doing for another weekend. Showering in hotels was nice, but not the same as at home. I had always loved being home. With what little motivation I had left, I moved Reagan's freshly re-washed towels to the dryer and threw my first load of clothes in the washer. Somehow, I'd subconsciously thought to plug my phone in before crashing hard in my bed.

I couldn't make sense of my dreams as the disjointed storylines jumped from one to another. The only common theme among them was the faint sound of a familiar song streaming from Kendrick's lips. It's definitely a song that was released before either of us was born, so where do I know that song from? I was woken by a crash coming from somewhere in the apartment, and I could still hear the same song that had drifted into my dreams. Groggily, I dragged myself out of bed to check on the noise.

"Reagan?" My voice croaked as I squinted at the lights.

"I'm sorry, I was trying so hard to be quiet," she apologized before wrapping her arms around me into a hug. "Gosh, I missed you while you were in Ireland. Welcome home."

"What are you doing?" My brain wasn't awake enough to make much sense of anything except the nagging feeling to go back to sleep.

"I was trying to prepare dough to make those homemade cinnamon rolls that you like so much," she admitted as she released me from her grip. "I wanted to surprise you with a nice breakfast in the morning since you spent all day traveling. I guess the cat's out of the bag though since I couldn't pull out the pan without making so much noise." It finally registered that Reagan's phone was lying on the kitchen counter, playing music at full volume. "I Was Made for Lovin' You" by Kiss was still playing, nearing the end of the repetitive seven-minute song. She followed my gaze to her phone, suddenly realizing how loud her music must have been. "I'll turn this down and finish up in here. By the way, I moved my towels from the dryer, so you can go ahead and move your clothes over if you want."

Though I felt like a zombie, I did just that, mentally patting myself on the back for washing the load that wouldn't wrinkle if left in the dryer most of the night. By the time I returned to my bed, I could no longer hear music or anything that would disrupt the much-needed rest my body demanded. Instead of dreaming about late 70s music, my mind conjured up legends of leprechauns and enchanted stones.

CHAPTER TWO

"Every time I see you here I forget that Kendrick gave you a spare key," Mikey said as he joined me on their penthouse balcony. He sat in the chair across from mine rather than one of the two next to me. Reagan and I living a few floors below was the reason Kendrick invested in four chairs and a table for their balcony.

"I brought Reagan's homemade cinnamon rolls with me if that's any consolation," I offered by way of apology for not letting him know ahead of time. I'd thoroughly needed that vacation time, but I'd missed the views of this city. The air was somewhat humid, as it tended to be during summers here, but we weren't far enough into summer yet for the heat to usher me into air-conditioned rooms.

"I still don't understand why you like coming up here to an empty balcony when there's a perfectly good pool that's now open for the season," Mikey shook his head as he stretched back on his chair.

I mirrored his movements and said, "The keyword is 'empty.' While I do relish opportunities to people-watch, I've spent entirely too much time around people for the past week and a half. I had to share a hotel room with my sister and brother, which meant zero alone time, and you know how delicate we introverts are without our alone time to recharge."

Mikey, much like his cousin Kendrick, was an extrovert through and through. Mikey was on a different level though, the life of the party. Only recently did he start to mellow a bit with some maturity. His eyes were the same blue as Kendrick's, the kind of ocean eyes that girls fawn over and Billie Eilish sings about. He was a few inches taller than Kendrick and lankier as a result, but some of his scrawniness had filled out since the two made regular trips to the gym after moving into One Light. Perhaps if I hadn't known Kendrick first, I could consider dating someone like Mikey, but there was no way of knowing what could or would have been. Mikey and Reagan, however...

"What do you think of my roommate Reagan?" I abruptly asked. Great, that was subtle, and not at all something I had wanted to say out loud even though it was one of life's great mysteries that constantly made its rounds in my head.

"I think she's nice," he hedged carefully, seeming to debate how much he wanted to disclose to me. After a few seconds, he relented. "She's also smart, hot, and a lot of fun to be around. But I don't think she's interested in a serious relationship right now. I don't want to get emotionally invested in someone who may not be marriage material yet."

Marriage material? "Marriage material?" I asked in an echo to my thoughts.

"You live with her, so you know how she is sometimes," he tried to say in defending himself. "Reagan is one of your best friends and your roommate, and my cousin and roommate is your other best friend. If I date Reagan and it doesn't work out, it might make things awkward between the four of us. When people dating within the same friend circle break up, often sides are taken. That wouldn't be fair to you and Kendrick. I'm not saying that I'm not interested in her, but with the way Reagan acts around me, I can't see a relationship lasting long-term because I would want things to move faster than she's ready for. Maybe in a few months, I'll feel differently about her and the future. I'm getting too old to waste time dating someone just because."

Everything he said made perfect sense to me. If Reagan and I hadn't been stuck together as freshmen in the college dorms, I'd probably see her as a flight risk when it comes to long-term commitments and planning. Fortunately, she had gotten better over the years, especially once she stopped changing majors. Without an academic scholarship, there was a fair chance she would have joined the circus instead of going to college just to see if she could. Secretly, I admired her bravery when it came to taking risks. When taking all the friendship intricacies into account, it was no wonder Mikey had never acted on his attraction. I couldn't blame him when I had been doing the same when it came to Kendrick, and I knew things would likely work out with Kendrick if he felt the same way.

"You and Kendrick, however, have a high probability of lasting a lifetime," Mikey said, seeing through every denial

I'd thrown his way when he had brought this up in the past. "I understand that you've been friends forever and you don't want to lose that, but hear me out. One of you is going to find someone else sooner or later, and it'll probably be Kendrick, but only because he's actually putting himself out there to an extent. Truth is, your friendship won't be the same once one of you starts considering a life with someone else. If Sarah hadn't moved away, it would have happened already. Ariella, I think you should take the risk and tell him how you feel."

"But what if he doesn't feel the same way?" I voiced my fear, hoping that Mikey might have an answer I hadn't already thought of.

"Then it's awkward for a while," he shrugged. "But time will pass and you'll both move past it. At least then you'll know and be able to move on and find someone even better."

"Better than Kendrick?" I doubted such a human existed, but I went along with Mikey's scenario.

"He is pretty great, isn't he? It must run in the family. I'm sure we have other cousins who would love to visit and take you out on a date. At least think about it. I'm gonna go eat my share of the cinnamon rolls before Kendrick comes home and devours them all."

I rolled my eyes at his suggestion to set me up with another cousin of theirs but seriously contemplated the ramifications of admitting all this to Kendrick. Both the best-case and worst-case scenarios would complicate things. Scratch that, there was no scenario in which things weren't complicated, including the one where I'd have to watch him fall in love with someone who wasn't me. A decision didn't need to be made right now.

I waited until Mikey was in his room to go inside and sneak back to my apartment, wanting to avoid running into Kendrick before Monday. By Monday, I needed to figure out if telling him was something I wanted. Now was the perfect time to stop procrastinating, buy my groceries for the week, and forget about Kendrick for a few hours.

One thing I wouldn't miss about apartment life when I had my own house was the logistics of carrying my groceries from the trunk of my car to my apartment. The elevator helped to an extent, but my arms could only hold so many bags for the distance from my car to said elevator and from the elevator to my kitchen. Leaving either my car or my apartment unlocked was technically unsafe if more than one trip was required. Kendrick and I tried to coordinate our shopping runs together to lessen the load and save on gas. With the two of us, one trip to each apartment covered all the bags. All of those were facts that I had forgotten about until I shifted my car into park with a trunk full of food and necessities and no Kendrick around to help. I could call Mikey and see if he was around to help but not if his help meant more conversations about things I'd rather avoid for as long as possible. The added exercise would be good for me.

Without the aid of my best friend and his muscles, my groceries required three trips up the elevator. By the time I'd finished putting everything in its assigned place, I had two missed calls and a text from Kendrick.

KENDRICK

It just crossed my mind that you probably need to stock up on groceries given that you've been out of town. I'll be home around 4 if you want to go today.

Too little too late. I just finished unpacking. This experience has taught me that while you slow me down when we're going through the store due to your refusal to make a list, it takes almost twice as long to carry it all up.

KENDRICK

Are you admitting that you use me for my muscle? I'll have you know that I'm very capable of making a grocery list and sticking to it. I happen to enjoy the spontaneity of discovering new items at the store that I would have never come across if all I did was stick to a list.

You're a guy and I'm a girl; of course, I use you for your muscle. Why do you think I insisted that we should live in the same apartment building? You're only a few floors away if I need someone to kill a spider or open a tight jar.

And here I thought our friendship was the reason you wanted me close ;)

I don't see how your muscle isn't considered a valid part of our friendship. We might not still be friends if you weren't a strong guy willing to help. Don't act as if you don't enjoy how our friendship affects the cleanliness of your kitchen.

On more than one occasion when Kendrick and Mikey decided to host game night in their penthouse, I was the one wiping down counters and steam mopping their floors both before and after their guests. For two bachelors sharing an apartment, they did a decent job cleaning up after themselves, but neither of them seemed to see the value in spending $100 for a mop that would both disinfect and dry quickly. I had yet to find a vacuum anywhere in that penthouse either. Apparently, a girl taking the elevator up with a vacuum and steam mop was a strange enough occurrence to warrant looks from other residents, though I knew some of them likely hired a cleaning service for their apartments rather than cleaning it on their own. And by some, I knew at least the resident professional football player who lived in one of the other penthouse suites hired a cleaning service. I would too if I had his kind of money.

KENDRICK

One of these days I'm going to surprise you by returning the favor. I'll have to Google how to use a vacuum and steam mop, but it can't be that difficult, right?

I'll believe it when I see it.

"Are you texting Kendrick?" Reagan said behind me, causing me to jump. I was too engrossed in my phone to hear the front door open.

"Why do you ask that?" My words came across more defensively than I had intended.

"You get a goofy look on your face every time you text him," she said bluntly. "Don't worry though, he's too oblivious to notice the way you look at him, and he doesn't know the way you talk about him. I can't tell whether he's ignorant by choice though."

Exasperated from having already talked to Mikey about Kendrick earlier, I replied, "Fine, whatever, can we please talk about something other than Kendrick?"

"Well, I was hoping that you would tell me about your trip," Reagan admitted, sitting down at one of our two barstools. "You were so exhausted last night, and I had to work earlier today. Tell me everything and show me all the pictures. I want enough details that I can visit Ireland vicariously through you."

I perched myself on the other barstool and opened the photos app on my phone, scrolling up to find the beginning of the trip. I described the whole ordeal, going in chronological order from the first flight to Chicago O'Hare to the rush to reach the gate for our final flight back to Kansas City. Going through customs arriving in Ireland was a stark contrast to the line for customs when returning to the U.S. I had heard it was even easier when visiting countries such as Italy. All they did was ask why you were there, and once you told them it was for tourism, they let you go on your merry way because that was one of the largest industries for them.

"Americans must stick out like a sore thumb in these countries," Reagan theorized from what little I had disclosed to her so far. "Not just the way we talk, but also our culture and the way we carry ourselves. And in Ireland, the dialects could easily pinpoint an American, British, Australian, or any other English-speaking native. It's fascinating how accents of the same base language can vary, even within a country like ours."

"From what I understand, smaller countries than ours have the same type of variances," I said, remembering things I had studied in a college course. "If I have my facts straight, the Italian language as it's taught is essentially all the dialects, which is why some words in English have more than one word in Italian. I've even heard that those from southern regions near Sicily can't understand parts of the Venetian dialect, and Italy isn't that large of a country."

"Anyway, back to your adventures in Ireland," Reagan said, eager to get on with the story. Telling these things to her was a good practice round for sharing with Kendrick and any other coworkers who would ask. She would ask questions and details that most wouldn't feel comfortable voicing, except for Kendrick. Now that I thought about it, Mikey hadn't asked about Ireland, but I hadn't given him much opportunity to either. Maybe Kendrick would share the condensed versions of what I disclosed in the way that guys tell things to each other. I would pay money to overhear conversations those two have about either Reagan or me.

Reagan sighed and admired the many photos I'd taken, admitting that she was slightly jealous that she hadn't planned her own overseas vacation for the summer. "Vacations require both planning and money," I reminded her jokingly. Realistically, if one had enough money, not much planning would be required for such escapades. Also, if hostels were used rather than a decent hotel, one could get away with spending less. Reagan tended to avoid planning, which was why she spent her vacation days on road trips with her dad. Sometimes I wondered if she purposely didn't take other trips so she could have that time with her dad.

"Mark my words, I will go on a trip to Europe next year, even if it means eating peanut butter and jelly sandwiches for lunch every day starting tomorrow," she declared with determination. I never knew which times to believe her because sometimes, she would follow through. Last fall, she ran a half marathon after months of training. After that, she decided that completing the full marathon was a bit of a stretch.

"In that case, you might need to go buy bread," I pointed out since the bread I had bought was my favorite cinnamon raisin bread for my breakfast. "And probably peanut butter and jelly while you're at it."

Reagan pulled her phone out of her pocket as if to type a list. If she started buying more groceries, it would mean fewer styrofoam takeout containers filling the trash or taking up space in the fridge. It could potentially mean grocery runs becoming a three-person outing. I wasn't sure if I was ready or willing to give up that precious alone time with Kendrick. Now, if I could convince both her and Mikey to go together...

"You could see if Mikey wants to grab groceries with you," I hinted to her. "Kendrick should be getting home about now, and he hasn't gone to the store yet either."

She considered my idea for a moment and told me, "That could work. But don't you dare start matchmaking. I've watched enough rom-coms to know that it never works."

"Actually, matchmaking tends to go over fairly well in rom-coms. Are you admitting that you would give Mikey a chance if he showed interest?" I asked with a good guess as to the answer. Reagan was subtle, skilled in the art of "playing it cool," but I was also skilled in observation.

Whether or not the two were willing to admit it to each other, anyone who looked closely at their interactions could see the sparks between them.

"Mikey isn't the kind of guy that you merely give a chance to," Reagan said, her words confusing me until she finished her thought. "Mikey is the kind of guy that you make serious commitments with. He's fun and the life of the party, but he's also intentional when it comes to his future, which is why I doubt he sees me that way. I haven't been the best at following through with my goals when it comes to my career and planning for the future. I'm a bit more of a free spirit than he would probably prefer."

"Has it ever occurred to you that maybe Mikey sees you that way because that's the way you present yourself to him? From my observations, you tend to exaggerate certain aspects of your personality when you're around him as a way to keep him at arm's length. Why don't you try letting your walls down a little?" I asked, knowing it might be crossing a line. Questions like that ventured into the realm of a possible fight or conflict depending on the other's reaction.

She didn't seem upset though; rather, she seemed thoughtful. With most people, it was a good sign when anger wasn't immediately showing. "It's easier to seem carefree and bulletproof in the dating world than to be serious and vulnerable," she responded. "But it would be nice to have a guy see all the sides to my personality. Just because I'm spontaneous doesn't mean I don't want a husband and kids one day."

"Not that it would matter to someone like Mikey or any other decent guy," I started, attempting to choose my words carefully, "but your current job situation doesn't help much either. You have a college degree in teaching, and instead of looking for a job as a teacher like you say you will, you're waiting tables and working double shifts on the weekend. Granted, teachers aren't paid as much as they should be, but at least you would have benefits and a regular schedule. I don't think you want to be working in a restaurant for the rest of your life, even if the tips are good. If you do though, that's completely your decision to make. Work is work."

"Do you think that I'm avoiding going after what I want?"

Tread carefully signs flashed in my vision. "Yes, but I think it's because you're scared to think or plan for the future. You're incredibly smart and would make a great teacher when you finally decide to go after it. I know it was disappointing when you didn't find a teaching position right out of college, but it's almost as if you've given up rather than trying again. Rejection hurts, but you can't live in it forever."

Reagan's expression could be compared to that of a lost puppy. Telling someone the truth they needed to hear was hard, and the difficulty was magnified based on how close your relationship was. Since we graduated college and moved into this apartment, watching Reagan's job search had been like watching someone tread water—staying afloat without going anywhere. She made enough to pay her share of the bills, but it was hard to save up for emergencies or anything extra. My first year after college was similar, but we both learned how to budget and cut expenses when necessary. I hated watching her struggle to get ahead financially.

"I'm gonna go ask Mikey and Kendrick about going to Target," Reagan said, failing to hide the tint of sadness in her voice. "I can't imagine that they would reject the opportunity to tag along, given their typical love for food."

Once I heard the front door close and lock, I pulled ingredients out of the fridge to prepare my dinner and lunches for the next few days. The earlier I ate, the earlier I could go to bed. If only there were a cure for jet lag.

CHAPTER THREE

The adventures of Kendrick and Ariella—my mother's reference for our friendship—began during our freshman year of high school. To be more exact, our first encounter was before the first bell rang on the first day of school, since our assigned lockers were neighboring each other. If that had been our only time together, we would have been acquaintances at the most, but sharing the same homeroom, lunch period, English, and drama classes all contributed to the fantasy in my teenage head that the cute guy sitting next to me a few times a day was destined to be mine. His dark hair and blue eyes gave me a reason to show up for all the mundaneness and turbulence that surrounded my teenage existence.

Of course, I had the confidence level of the average high school freshman while Kendrick was unusually sure of himself in a way that constantly caught the attention of the more popular girls at school. I quickly settled into my role as the best friend, content to be the confidant and soundboard for his confusion over high school girls. Although my place in his life meant I could never admit my feelings for him, it held more permanence than the girlfriends who merely lasted a few months or weeks. Margie might have been the girl he danced with at our senior year homecoming dance, but I was the one he collaborated with when sending college applications and scheduling campus tours. His refusal to land himself in a long-distance relationship was how we volunteered to go to prom together as friends.

Remaining in the friend zone was the only sure way to end up at college together in the same general education lectures and late-night coffee runs while cramming for an exam. Even when our courses differed with our chosen majors—his being civil engineering while I pursued a degree in marketing—we would still schedule library study dates as a way to keep each other accountable. The few guys who did make any attempt to pursue me had tried and failed to get in the way of my friendship with Kendrick. When given the ultimatum "me or Kendrick," I willingly walked away and out of the relationship. Sarah, his only consistent girlfriend during his undergrad years, didn't seem to mind how much time Kendrick and I spent together. When her schedule aligned with ours, she would join us in the library for study sessions. If she was jealous, she never outwardly expressed it. If I hadn't harbored any feelings for my best friend, I would have been upset for them when they broke up at our college graduation. Four years hadn't changed his rule about long-distance relationships, and Sarah had been accepted into a medical school in New York. Once again, we had stepped into a new phase of life together, both of us single.

Just as we had with our college essays, Kendrick and I took turns helping each other with resumes and job applications. No longer were we on the university campus buying caffeine from the library coffeehouse, but rather, we were sharing a pot of coffee brewed at one of our apartments to stay within our adult budgets. In a way that coincidentally felt like destiny again, we were both hired by the same company, though in different departments. Street and Sons Engineering became our home away from home as Kendrick settled into the role of a civil project engineer while I found myself knee-deep in marketing proposals.

What I didn't foresee is how adding the label of *co-worker* could make it even more difficult to inch my way out of the friend zone. On the other hand, engineering was an industry that was still male-dominant and our company was no different. Nightmares of witnessing female coworkers attempt to flirt with Kendrick were non-existent due to the majority of his department consisting of men. In fact, I was currently the only female at the company who wasn't married or in a committed relationship; however, there were several good options in the dating pool for me. If you could call guys who never made a move legitimate options.

Perhaps one of the greatest advantages of working in the same building with my best friend was tied to the fact that we lived in the same apartment building. We could each drive to work or even carpool together, but the addition of the streetcar along Main Street (also known as trolley cars in other areas or trams in Europe) gave us means of alternative transportation for our morning and evening commutes. During the winter months of dark mornings and darker evenings, I had my own bodyguard to ensure my safety. On an ordinary day, Kendrick wouldn't hurt a fly; however, I did not doubt that he would come to my aid if I were ever in any danger.

Per our Monday morning routine, he was already waiting for me in the apartment building lobby with two coffee cups in his hands. "Top o' the mornin' to ya!" he greeted me with a smile that melted the heart of every girl in the vicinity and an appalling Irish accent that made the guy within earshot wince. It was so horribly cheesy that I couldn't help but roll my eyes.

"The only reason I'm letting you get away with that is the coffee in your hand," I said as he handed me my favorite caffeinated beverage. June or December, there's nothing that compares to the first sip of hot coffee in the early hours of the day. "I might need two more of these to stave off the leftover jet lag from the flight back."

"How was it?" he asked expectantly, holding the door open as we walked onto the sidewalk.

"What a loaded question. Let me start from the beginning." It took me a moment to register that I'd said all that out loud, not just the part I'd meant to say. It didn't seem to phase Kendrick though, and he gave me an attentive expression. "I tried to sleep as much as possible on the flight there since that's when we would be losing time and arriving in the morning. The jet lag was still brutal, but fortunately, Ireland is one of the many European countries that enjoys coffee. I did have to make the extra effort to make sure I was ordering a coffee without whiskey. That was a continual problem throughout the whole trip."

"You have to admit that trying it would have been fun," he insisted.

I glared at him before continuing. "It takes a while to adjust to the accents there as well. I knew it wouldn't be as easy to pick up on as British or Australian accents, but sometimes I wonder if their English dialect is a whole separate language in itself. I guess Scottish accents are also harder to understand."

"But you had fun, right?" he asked as we stepped onto the stopped streetcar and found two seats together.

"We stood in line to kiss a rock that millions of other people have also kissed," I said matter-of-factly. "It's completely unsanitary, though, I'm sure the rain and sun help reduce the germs that would build up there over the centuries. I let Kathleen go first just in case."

"Sounds like a great way to spread an infectious disease. You did kiss the Blarney Stone though, right? It would be like you to stand in line to kiss some random rock no one has ever heard of." I rolled my eyes at him before pulling out my phone to show him the one video Kathleen had taken on our trip, proof that I had tried something new. His expression was slightly scrutinizing, as though he were inspecting my face. "I knew there was something different about you. Must be that Gift of Eloquence. You're not as talkative as I anticipated though."

"I'm sorry to disappoint. Did I mention that I spent a third of the flight back trying to convince the lady next to me that most of Kansas City is in Missouri? Yes, there is a Kansas City, Kansas, but the parts that people think of, including the international airport, Kauffman Stadium, and

Arrowhead Stadium, are all on the Missouri side. It doesn't help that the state's two largest cities both share metro areas with a neighboring state."

If I had stopped my ranting soapbox for long enough, I would have noticed the thoughtful look on Kendrick's face as he listened to one of my pet peeves. It was one thing for a foreigner not to realize what state a certain city might be in when a different state's name was in the city's name—New York City, Oklahoma City, and Indianapolis are all obvious as to which state they're in—but Americans have no excuse to be ignorant about the geography of their own country. Not to mention Americans who didn't know how to properly speak their own language, let alone any others. This was why many other nations made fun of Americans.

"My commute was boring without you here," Kendrick said, standing in anticipation of our approaching stop. He turned to give me a hand up as the doors slid open. Like the gentleman he was, he opened the doors for me at the entrance to our office building. While most of our coworkers were typically friendly enough to greet me in the morning, today each one of them took the time to welcome me back from my vacation. Some of them probably needed my assistance with something and had been waiting patiently for my return. I was sure a select few were starting to be annoyed by the pile that had accumulated at my desk. I would belong to the second group had the tables been turned.

"Nice to have you back, Ariella," my boss said as he passed in a hurried walk toward the restrooms. Li Jun Street's father had started the company nearly fifty years ago and had passed ownership down to his son, half-Chinese from his mother's side, a decade ago. Those who had been at the company long enough to have experienced the transition from father to son often told stories of the company's founder and how the apple didn't fall far from the tree. The similarities shared between the two provided a sense of continuity and stability to the employees. People were creatures of habits and patterns, and the current boss was no different. Until Kendrick appeared in the lobby as if waiting for someone, I would have assumed today was another normal Monday.

Any innocent bystander would have looked at me and thought I was concentrating on whatever project was on my computer screen. The angle of my monitor gave me the perfect view to discreetly admire Kendrick and the way his shirt today deepened the azure of his eyes. If Mikey was right and Kendrick did find himself a girlfriend soon, I would no longer be free to see him this way without causing some serious issues for myself. Kendrick wasn't mine, and the only way to make that possible would be to tell him. If I could kiss an unhygienic rock while half-suspended in the air, I could make this leap.

Before I could do something or say something that would make it impossible to change my mind, Kendrick greeted a guy I had never seen before. In a split second, my eyes shifted to the face of the stranger, a face that rivaled Kendrick's handsomeness. His olive skin, green eyes, and neatly styled dark curls combined with the lack of a ring on his left hand sent warning signals to my brain. It was fairly common for clients to stop by for meetings or to talk to one of the engineers.

"Welcome back, Luca. Looks like you made the cut," I overheard Kendrick say to the stranger who must have been Luca. *Made the cut?*

Li Jun burst into the lobby with full vivacity, "Luca! Good to have you joining us. Kendrick, show Luca to the empty desk next to yours. Our IT Specialist should be here any minute to help set up your new workstation. Ariella," my boss turned to me to give instructions, "we'll need to order a new name badge for Luca's desk. We've hired him as one of our new Project Managers."

Not a client, but a coworker. He must have come in and gone through interviews during the time I was in Ireland. Unless Kendrick had known that Luca was officially hired, he wouldn't have thought to warn me. Because Kendrick was a guy likely unaware of how attractive Luca was, he probably wouldn't have thought to warn me even if he did know. Once they had walked away, I managed to refocus on wading through the pile of work in front of me.

"Oh, to be single again and have a chance at that," Hannah said to no one in particular from her desk to my right. "Then again, I don't know how I'd get anything done at home if I were married to someone who looks like Luca or even Kendrick." I'd just lost ten minutes of valuable time while they were both within my eyesight, so her analysis might not be far off from the truth.

Sometimes when Hannah made comments out loud, I would indulge her by responding, but my post-vacation workload was a bit too much for multitasking. Still, my mouth moved of its own accord, "I would think it would take discipline and adopting the 'work hard, play hard' mentality."

She smiled at me before she answered the phone. Given that my longest relationship had only lasted two months, I had no idea what I was talking about half the time when she was waiting for a response. The closest I could get was trying to imagine what it would be like if I were dating or married to Kendrick, but even that fell short. He and I had been friends long enough that we were comfortable with each other on a level that new couples took months to achieve. I wouldn't need to date him for years to be sure about a future with him because I already knew him.

At lunch, I warmed up my leftovers from last night's dinner in the break room microwave before I sat in my usual seat. Instead of one, I heard two chairs near me being moved and looked up to see Luca sitting down next to Kendrick. Any chance I had at a private lunch break conversation with Kendrick vanished the same way my train of thought did when Luca smiled at me. "You must be Ariella," he said as he stretched out his hand to offer me a handshake. I accepted and shook his hand, trying to hide how nervous his presence made me feel. Almost belatedly, I nodded to confirm his assumption.

"I'm the new guy, Luca, as everyone probably knows by now," he said as his introduction.

"News travels fast around here," Kendrick added jokingly, though the statement was true. Our company had less than 50 employees, which meant that everyone knew each other on some level. Our company could be twice the size as it was now, yet Luca wouldn't have been able to go unnoticed, at least to the women.

"I recently moved here from Chicago," Luca told us as he unwrapped his sandwich from saran wrap. "Most of my extended family lives there, including my parents and grandparents, and it was hard to live my life separate from their expectations. My grandparents immigrated from Italy, and much of the culture is still ingrained in them. So, I decided to move far enough away that they can't drop by anytime they feel like it, but close enough that I can drive, fly, or take the Amtrak train if I want to see them."

"How do your parents feel about your moving a state away?" I couldn't help but ask. As much as I needed my space from my own family, I couldn't imagine having to drive more than the two hours that I currently would drive to my parents' house. With both Kathleen and I living in Kansas City, our parents were usually the ones making the trip here to see both of us. Having an older sister nearby helped ease any misgivings they may have had about two daughters living in the city unsupervised.

"They were surprisingly supportive," Luca answered. "Well, it probably helps that I'm not the oldest or the youngest of my siblings. My younger brother is living at home while attending college. My sister is the oldest, and she did us all a favor by getting married promptly following her college graduation. A few months ago, she gave birth to their first grandchild. Babies take away any once overbearing attention."

We had the middle child fact in common, but it sounded as if there were a difference in family dynamics, likely due to cultural variances. The contrast in our personalities, from what I had observed during our limited interactions, played a role as well. Luca didn't strike me as the type content to fade into the shadows, but rather the type who longed to escape limiting expectations to create his own path. My path had always been the path of least resistance.

"I have a hard time imaging any of my sisters having a baby," Kendrick piped up, his mouth partially full of his leftover pizza.

"Your sisters are all younger than you," I pointed out to him. Kendrick was the only boy and the oldest in his family. Having all younger sisters was likely what influenced the sensitive and protective side of him that I benefited from.

Kendrick responded to me, "Fine, then I have a hard time imagining your older sister having a baby."

"I can't disagree with that," I said with a shrug. I had a hard time picturing her married, let alone being responsible for a vulnerable human. The problem hadn't been Kathleen as much as it was her choice of boyfriends. I had tried time and time again to picture a future with my sister married to Sullivan, but I had never been able to see it last. A lifetime of Sullivan O'Hare as a permanent fixture in my family was unsettling, no matter how many times he picked us up from the airport.

"My sister has always loved babies," Luca said. "It was surprising that they waited as long as they did after the wedding. She and her husband will likely end up with a large family."

"What's your definition of a large family?" I asked Luca, my curiosity having gotten the best of me. My parents had three children, and that seemed like plenty to me. I had only known a handful of families with more kids than that, and they usually had to buy larger minivans or those big twelve-passenger vans that didn't get decent miles per gallon. I wouldn't want to have to drive anything larger than the Prius I currently owned.

Both the guys pondered my question as if they had never seriously thought about how many children were considered a large family. Kendrick offered an answer first. "Once you have more than two, you're outnumbered. More than three means that you can't fit your family in a regular sedan car, but many SUVs have the option of adding an extra row in exchange for trunk space. A lack of trunk space isn't helpful though if all your kids are playing sports that require gym bags in addition to backpacks. My final answer is more than three children." Kendrick and I turned our gazes expectantly to Luca in anticipation of his answer.

"I'm going to go with five or more," Luca admitted before defending his answer. "I prefer even numbers, and three children often means one of them gets left out, usually whichever one is a different gender from the other two. Maybe if all three were the same gender, it's less likely that someone would get left out, but it's rare to see that in a family. Two doesn't seem like enough, so four would be an ideal number." At that moment of the conversation, I remembered that I was talking to two males, neither of whom would have to be the ones going through a forty-week pregnancy followed by labor for each child. "As the only female representation, what do you think a large family consists of?" I fought to keep a blush from creeping up my spine as both sets of eyes focused on me.

"I have to agree with Kendrick, but I'm not a fan of driving larger vehicles," I said with a shrug. "Maybe I would feel differently about minivans parking in an attached garage versus the parking lot or parking garage of an apartment complex, but there would still be the issue of finding parking in public places. Too many people who have a license don't know how to properly maneuver their vehicles between the allotted lines. It's one of the reasons that I utilize public transportation to commute to work when there isn't ice or snow or frigid temperatures." There was a day last winter when I stubbornly insisted that Kendrick and I suck it up and take our usual means to the office. The air had been so bitterly cold that I begged Kendrick to go back to the apartment during his lunch break and get his car so we wouldn't have to travel home by walking and riding the streetcar.

"I guess you're part of the fortunate minority who can use Kansas City's public transportation system without it being a large inconvenience," Luca surmised. "I'm sure the addition of the streetcar has helped some, but larger cities like Chicago have decent train systems. Having a car is very convenient though since any kind of public transportation requires following a schedule and knowing which direction to travel. I can see why car size and efficiency would be a deciding factor when having children in any city. Finances and the size of the house would also affect final decisions."

As Luca and Kendrick conversed about the advantages and disadvantages of various car models and makes, I dismissed myself to continue catching up on work. In hindsight, if I had to choose a third wheel in that lunch conversation, I wouldn't be able to decide who it was. Luca certainly wasn't unwelcome, and a lunch break at work wouldn't have been the best time for a serious conversation with Kendrick. Finding the right time might prove itself to be a bigger challenge than I previously foresaw.

CHAPTER FOUR

"Li Jun certainly has an eye for finding potential," Kendrick expressed as we rushed onto the stopped streetcar headed north toward home. I didn't know how some enjoyed living in larger cities like New York City where the subway systems seemed to go in every which direction and there were five major boroughs to get lost in. I was satisfied with my life in the heartland, in a city that offered both a sense of community and things to do. I was only half listening to Kendrick's appraisal of Luca's first day. "He has a lot of experience for someone in his twenties, though it helps that he's already gotten his professional engineering license. He had started going through the comity process to get his Missouri license before moving, which is what likely set him apart when he was interviewing. You know how Li Jun appreciates initiative. What did you think of Luca?"

"I think he's very attractive," I said without thinking. Kendrick appeared shocked with a mix of something else. Disappointment, maybe. But why would Kendrick be disappointed in what I thought of Luca? He was the one singing the guy's praises only seconds ago.

"I mean—" he stammered a bit as he grasped for words, "I guess he's a good-looking guy, objectively speaking." The air between us was awkward and uncomfortable, but before I could concoct something to break the silence, our stop was announced. On the way out, Kendrick accidentally bumped into a couple who had been kissing and not paying attention to their surroundings. The only thing I caught of the scene was the strange look on Kendrick's face as if he recognized one of them, but he hurried me forward so that we wouldn't hold up the streetcar.

"What's wrong?" I asked, wanting to kick myself for not being more specific. More than one thing had occurred that could be wrong, and the conversation about Luca was the one I would rather avoid hashing out at the moment.

Kendrick didn't respond right away, and I wondered if he had even heard my question. We continued walking the short distance from the stop to the apartment building. When we were alone in the elevator, he finally acknowledged my concern. "That guy who was on the streetcar looked just like Kathleen's boyfriend, but that wasn't Kathleen that he was nearly groping on public transportation. Maybe I was just seeing things or he might have a brother who looks a lot like him, but the way he looked at me made it seem as if he also recognized me."

My mind was reeling as I struggled to make sense of this tidbit of information. Sullivan, the guy whom I have never trusted despite his best efforts, might have been cheating on my sister. Part of me wanted to use the excuse that it could have been someone who looked like him, which was possible according to theories about doppelgängers. I wasn't sure if Sullivan had any brothers or cousins who might share similar enough features to be mistaken for him. While I refused to jump to conclusions based on a split-second moment that I didn't witness myself, my intuition suspected that Kendrick was right. Kendrick and Sullivan had only met a handful of times, but Kendrick was the type to remember a face. Intuition alone wasn't enough to bring this up with my sister though.

"What do I do?" I asked Kendrick, hoping he had thought of a solution during the walk from the streetcar to the elevator.

"I don't know," he resigned as he pulled me into a side hug. "I know that you've always felt something was off about him, but unless we have solid evidence that he's cheating, it's not worth involving yourself in your sister's relationship."

Proof sounded like something out of a detective movie, reminiscent of my Nancy Drew obsession growing up. If that was Sullivan, there had to be a way to expose him somehow. Kissing someone else in public like that wasn't exactly a discreet way to cover up any transgressions. Kathleen traveled for work sometimes, which would leave opportunities to spy on him since he checked on her cat while she was gone. First, though, I needed to eliminate some of the other possibilities.

Hey, does Sullivan have any brothers or cousins who live in the area?

After I sent the message to my sister, I opened Facebook to check Sullivan's profile page for linked family members or tagged photos with family. I scrolled through, but the only other male in the photos of his immediate family was a man who was unmistakably Sullivan's father. No cousins were featured in any photos or linked as family members, a dead end since social media rarely gave the whole family tree.

"Do I even want to know what you're doing?" Kendrick asked as he tugged me toward the open elevator door that had stopped at my floor.

"Trying to find out if Sullivan look-a-likes exist in his family," I said as if it were obvious. "I know so little about him that he could have a twin brother that no one has mentioned." Spying was a more far-fetched plan than checking for an identical twin. I had to eliminate the obvious possibilities before assuming the worst. I didn't want to let my unease about him cloud my judgment.

KATHLEEN

He has a sister, no brothers. I think he's the only boy in his family because it was a big deal when he was born since everyone else only had girls. Weird and random question, sis.

Kendrick took the initiative to unlock my door for me and make himself at home in my apartment as I checked my family's shared Google calendar for upcoming dates that Kathleen would be out of town. This coming Friday through Wednesday, her company was hosting an event in Boston. Bingo.

"Do you have plans on Friday night?" I asked Kendrick after returning my phone to my back pocket. Belatedly, it crossed my mind that he could have a date planned with one of the many girls who messaged him on his dating app.

He raised one eyebrow at me in question. "What am I about to agree to help you with?"

"You said we need solid evidence," I said to point out the logic of the idea before the crazy part, "so I was thinking that maybe we should follow Sullivan around for a while to see if he does anything suspicious to support what you think you saw today. Kathleen will be out of town for work Friday through Wednesday, and he usually stops by her apartment once or twice a day while she's gone."

"You want to spy on your sister's boyfriend? What if he notices us?" It wasn't an immediate no nor did he state anything about plans. Maybe he had given up on the girl he was supposed to go out with last Friday.

"Wigs and sunglasses," I said, more convinced once I'd heard the idea out loud. This plan could work.

Kendrick stared at a Chinese takeout menu on the counter in contemplation. "If I don't go with you, you'll do this without me, and if you get yourself hurt or in trouble, I'd hate myself for not being there to keep you safe. But we have to get realistic wigs, not the cheap Halloween ones. And if, after following him, we don't find anything, we should forget about it and let things play out on their own. He's likely to slip up at some point anyway if he's cheating in broad daylight."

"We have ourselves a deal," I said and stretched out my hand to shake his in agreement.

"Now, for our first order of business," Kendrick said, his attention back on the menu, "I'm treating you to Chinese food for dinner. I've been craving fried rice for a week now, but I know how upset you get when I order Chinese without you."

"I don't get upset," I argued, "but it's a much better investment to order for more than one person, especially if you're paying for delivery."

Kendrick pulled out his phone to call in the order even though I had shown him how to do it all through an app. As an introvert, I preferred using the app while his extroversion had no qualms about calling in the order. He ordered for me without asking, having memorized my go-to order during study nights in college. While he had a few favorite dishes, he sometimes liked to try something new when he was in a certain mood. Today, he ordered his usual General Tso's Chicken, maybe to balance out the craziness of my recent plan.

"Okay, we need to establish boundaries if we're going to do this," Kendrick said after confirming my address and hanging up. "At nine o'clock, we're done for the night, no exceptions. If we catch him with another girl, we have to get photos; I don't want to confront him about it when it's technically not my business. If he goes to a dangerous area of the city, we are not going to follow him. Last, but certainly not least, you are going to owe me big time for this escapade of yours, though it is a worthy cause. Your sister deserves better than someone who might be cheating on her. Oh, and maybe we should try using accents if we ever have to talk while he's around. He won't recognize my voice as much as yours, but I think it could be fun."

"Agreed. I've always wondered what I would look like with a blonde wig."

He paused at my comment as if he were picturing it in his mind. "Also, we have to let Reagan and Mikey know what we're doing and share our location with them, just in case anything sketchy happens," he added. "I think that should cover it. How are you going to tell her if it's true?"

"I'll cross that bridge when and if we get there," I said, as cliche as the phrase was. "There's no easy way to tell someone that their boyfriend is cheating, but I'd rather she hear it from me than catch him herself. I don't understand why people would even do it in the first place."

"Maybe people aren't fully satisfied in their current relationship when they find someone else. Instead of doing the brave thing—the right thing—they avoid breaking up because they either don't deal well with conflict, or they know they won't get everything they want or need out of either relationship. That's my only guess, anyway." I mulled over Kendrick's words and tried to gain a new perspective, some way to have compassion. While I understood what it was like to want to avoid conflict and maintain peace, cheating would cause too much inner turmoil to be worth the external peace.

While we waited for our food delivery, I showed Kendrick more photos from Ireland. I heard a knock at the door, and I opened it, assuming it would be the delivery person. Instead, Mikey and Reagan were standing in the hallway with their hands full of grocery bags while she was trying to fish her keys out of her bottomless purse.

"See, I told you it would be faster to knock," Mikey said to Reagan as he welcomed himself inside. I had assumed she had gone to the store last night when she'd left, but I hadn't noticed any additional food when making breakfast this morning. I would question her about where she went last night during that time, but with Mikey and Kendrick within earshot, I didn't want to expose her in case something else had come up. As Reagan followed Mikey inside, I saw a delivery worker appear in the elevator. Perfect timing. Well, perfect timing would have been before the roommates both showed up since we didn't order any food for them, but you couldn't have everything in life.

Mikey helped Reagan unpack her groceries as Kendrick unpacked our Chinese food. "See, I told you that it mattered how long we spent at the store," Mikey said to Reagan, referring to a conversation that must have happened at least an hour ago. "If we'd come back earlier, we either would have made it in time to put in our order for the delivery or we would have been in and out without knowing that we were left out of this glorious feast."

"I'd hardly call Chinese food a glorious feast," Kendrick said before taking a bite, "unless it's a Chinese buffet. This is the lazy version of that. That's the price of convenience."

The problem with buffets was the inability to have Chinese leftovers for several days afterward. The fried rice might have been a step up in quality when in the restaurant, but I could eat leftover fried rice every day and never tire of it. I had attempted to make my own several times, but it never tasted the same as what the restaurants serve. Still, it was no steak.

"I'm trying to stay within budget," Reagan reminded Mikey. "Since I just spent money on groceries, I shouldn't need to spend more money on Chinese food."

Mikey didn't respond, distracted by his phone. Without looking up from his screen, he asked her, "What kind of wings do you like? My treat. You shouldn't have to get groceries and cook on the same night." I looked over at Kendrick to gauge his reaction, but he was also on his phone. I felt a vibration from my phone and my smartwatch.

KENDRICK

No one should have to buy groceries and cook on the same day? I'm pretty sure plenty of functioning adults do that regularly. In some countries, they buy all their ingredients fresh that day before cooking them for dinner

Just let them have whatever moment is going on. I'm still surprised she followed through on buying food that needs to be cooked

It's not full adulting until she cooks the food that she bought. Meat that isn't cooked or frozen by a certain date is a waste of money

It'll be an even bigger waste if she cooks it and then doesn't eat most of it

"What private conversation are you two having over texting?" Reagan eyed us suspiciously.

"Well, it wouldn't be private if we told you about it, now would it?" Kendrick defended by answering her with another question. I fought back the embarrassment at Mikey's amused expression. The joke was on him though because he was also spending time with Reagan, and she might follow through with letting some of her walls down.

He returned his focus to his phone for a few more seconds before putting it away. "Let's go hang out in the penthouse," he said, the comment directed at Reagan. "I finally got ahold of a genuine Mario Kart for the Nintendo 64. The delivery driver is supposed to call me and meet me in the lobby when he arrives." Reagan peeked another look at Kendrick and me before exiting with Mikey.

I waited a few seconds after they had left before I asked Kendrick, "Why didn't you tell me that you now have Mario Kart 64? You know how much I loved playing that game growing up."

"Because you always beat me," he admitted with a shrug. "And I was a little distracted by everything that's happened today. You didn't need a distraction while trying to process the possible situation with Kathleen and Sullivan. Granted, maybe a video game would have kept you from concocting your wacky plan."

"I came up with that plan while we were on the elevator, so unless you had started the morning or our commute home with, 'Hey, want to play Mario Kart after work,' it would have prevented nothing," I stated my logical argument. "Now we have to wait until another night because if we go up there together, they'll think we're spying on them."

"So, it's okay to spy on Sullivan because we think he's cheating, but it's overstepping if we go to my own apartment where my cousin happens to be hanging out with your roommate?" he asked, and I knew he had made a solid point. I should have thought to go to the penthouse before we had ordered Chinese food so that we could eat it outside on the balcony instead of at my kitchen island. But then I wouldn't have witnessed Reagan and Mikey coming back from the grocery store together. "Come back to the here and now." There was a glint of playfulness in his eyes as he reminded me to focus on the present.

One of Kendrick's many gifts over the years of our friendship had been the way he recognized when my brain was lost on a tangent of *what ifs* and *should haves*. The older we became, the less often it happened, but he knew when I needed him to interrupt those thought processes.

On a broader level, Kendrick had always known when I needed him. The way I told the story, he and I had volunteered to go to senior year prom together, but the truth was, I had needed him. All the girls I was friends with then had dates, but no one bothered to try asking me. I wasn't bold enough to go by myself despite all that, and no girl wanted to be the one standing alone in all the photos. Although I had never told him how much I wanted to go, he must have figured it out somehow. He coordinated with my homeroom teacher and showed up to school early one morning to prepare his prom-posal. When I walked in, the normally clean whiteboard was decorated with colorful designs and script that read, "Ariella, will you go to prom with me? - Kendrick" right for all the class to see. A public ask like that was exactly what I didn't know I needed.

With a full stomach, the grogginess of a full day was catching up to me. I yawned as I rinsed the plates before putting them in the dishwasher. "Will the jet lag ever go away?" I complained, stifling another yawn.

"I should go and let you get ready for bed," Kendrick said and stood up from the stool. "Mondays are draining as it is, and you're still recovering from a transatlantic flight on top of that. Plus, it'll be much more subtle to spy on our roommates if it's just me rather than both of us."

He gave me whatever was leftover from our dinner and headed toward the door. I walked with him to say goodnight, closing and locking the door once he was gone. Now that I needed him to help spy on Sullivan O'Hare, I couldn't complicate our relationship with any confessions. Feelings would have to wait until after Friday night.

KENDRICK

They're just sitting on opposite sides of the sectional playing Mario Kart. Nothing suspicious to report. We're getting wigs after work tomorrow.

What Kendrick didn't recognize, in the way that most guys tended to miss, was that Mikey and Reagan spending time together as just the two of them was, in itself, suspicious. They had always gotten along well in groups or in instances where Kendrick and I dragged them along for an outing, but they had never taken the initiative to be alone with each other, even if they were on separate sides of the sectional. Having someone like Mikey show interest in Reagan might give her the push she needed to make the life changes she had been avoiding, and her showing her more responsible side was likely to encourage him to pursue her. If my interfering worked to my advantage, maybe the two of them becoming a couple could help show Kendrick that moving beyond friendship would ultimately be something incredible for the two of us.

CHAPTER FIVE

I checked and double-checked Kathleen's calendar multiple times per day throughout the week until I was certain that she had gotten on the plane for Boston. She had been tagged in a photo with a coworker on her company's social media page early Friday morning. Sullivan would likely wait until the evening to check on the cat before going off to do whatever he occupied his time with on weekends when my sister traveled.

Fortunately, Friday had already been designated a half day at our office in honor of Li Jun's father's birthday. Though Ben Street hadn't been the active president for years, he still stopped by several times a year, one of those days being his birthday. The company had lunch and a cake catered before closing the office for the remainder of the afternoon. It was a nice reprieve for me given that it was my first week back after a vacation, and I was certain Luca had similar feelings with it having been his first week working here. This might be a bit over-the-top, but it was tradition to at least have some type of dessert brought in for any employee's birthday.

It was one of those benefits that they never mentioned in interviews.

If I didn't need to be on my A-game tonight, I would have spent the better part of my afternoon soaking up Vitamin D at the apartment's rooftop pool, begging Kendrick every half hour or so to grab me a snack from his apartment. When you had hair that was so thick and long that it took nearly twenty-four hours to dry, going swimming only hours before putting on a wig wasn't a smart idea. What was a smart idea was taking advantage of the nearly empty game yard near the pool. During nice weather, the games seemed to attract more residents than the resort-style pool, but most others were still finishing their workweek. Around four or five was when this area would start to get crowded, and all the grills would be in use. Until then, Kendrick and I would have near privacy as we took advantage of our free afternoon.

So far, we were neck and neck playing cornhole. "Do you think we'll catch Sullivan cheating tonight?" I asked Kendrick, worried that all our efforts would be for nothing.

"I think it depends on if it was him on the streetcar on Monday," Kendrick said matter-of-factly. "If it was him, I think we shouldn't have any problems getting evidence. Someone who is that careless when their girlfriend is in town will be much more careless while she's away on the east coast. He has to know that you live around here and likely take the streetcar to work regularly."

"I hope you're right," I said, then refocused my attention on the goal. When the two of us played this game against our other friends (Mikey and Reagan more times than not), we dominated with our ability to play off each other's strengths. Times like this, one-on-one, called for longer matches to reach a winner. That, and the beautiful weather, was why Kendrick had insisted on coming out here rather than playing Mario Kart inside. Around four, as we had predicted, others emerged onto the game yard, with questions about the score and how long we had been playing this round. Most of them became invested in the game as they watched, making bets on which one of us would be the eventual victor. I overshot my last throw, which left me two points short of winning. Kendrick used my slip-up to his advantage and sealed the final win. Cheers erupted around us. Initially, I wondered if they were just waiting for their turn, but many congratulated Kendrick and gave their condolences to me. If winning put him in a better mood for tonight, I'd let him beat me at cornhole anytime. Well, maybe not every time, but anytime I needed a favor from him.

We went back inside to eat a snack before changing into our disguises for the evening. "Hey, can you add popcorn to your grocery list so that I remember to get some?" Kendrick asked as he put the last bag of his in the microwave.

"You know, you could just make your own list," I pointed out as I pulled out my phone to add it to my list. "It's not that difficult to keep a list on your phone in the Notes app. You can even set it to automatically open your list when you're near the grocery store. Technology makes some lazy, but it also removes a lot of excuses that people make."

Kendrick said, "Like the people who don't know how Do Not Disturb works. Or that you can set different alarms to go off automatically on varying days of the week if your wakeup time isn't always the same. Technology is at the point that if you're willing to pay, you can control your garage door with your phone as well as lock other doors in the house. Smartphones are highly underutilized for all the things they can do."

"Too bad we can't access Sullivan's location without permission," I sighed. "It would take some of the guesswork out of our mission. That would be an invasion of his privacy though."

"Stop whining and eat your popcorn," Kendrick teased, sitting next to me on the sectional. "He'll probably stop by your sister's place after work, so we need to make sure we're there by five to be safe, in case he got off work early. I still can't believe you talked me into this." He threw a piece of popcorn in the air and caught it with his mouth. I'd considered it a win anytime he didn't play with his food.

"I should have thought this through more," I admitted, suddenly having doubts about tonight. I was unnerved by the endless list of details that could go wrong with my plan. "I know what car he drives, and he has unique license plate covers, but it's not a small apartment complex. It might take us a while to find his car. We could miss him and not realize it."

"Ariella, it's going to be fine," he reassured me. "We can even hang out at the entrance to the parking garage and wait for him to drive inside. Or maybe we should be in the lobby close to the elevators so we can see when he leaves. It's up to you." He threw a piece of popcorn at me, but I caught it with my mouth.

I thought about the pros and cons of each option. The primary goal for our stakeout was to follow him to his next destination to see if our suspicions were true. The closer we were to his car, the better off we would be at keeping up with him when leaving the apartment complex. "We should stay in the parking garage once we find the SUV," I decided. "At the small chance that he has another girl with him instead of meeting one somewhere, he wouldn't bring her inside. The staff know both Sullivan and Kathleen and have seen them together enough to be suspicious about another girl with him."

His bowl now empty of his share of the popcorn, Kendrick had slowly inched his way closer to mine to steal handfuls from my bowl. When I side-eyed him, he said, "At the rate you're eating, none of the options will be relevant because he'll have arrived and left." I conceded and let him help himself to some of what I had left.

Thirty minutes later, we were in our sunglasses and wigs in Kendrick's car, driving the short distance from One Light to Two Light. I wouldn't put it past my sister to move to Three Light when they finished construction if she hadn't decided to relocate to a house in the suburbs by then. With how expensive one-bedroom apartments were at Two Light, I think it was a waste that she spent so much in rent every month, but the proximity to work was hard to reconcile. Time is money, after all. Kendrick used my guest pass to enter the secured parking, and he slowly inched forward as I examined all the vehicles. He drove around at a steady pace, but I only checked the license plates of SUVs that were of the same make and model as Sullivan's. Once we reached the top level, we started the descent back down to analyze any new arrivals.

"That's it!" I exclaimed when I recognized the tiny green leprechauns on the license plate cover. Kendrick did a quick scan for any nearby available spaces and parked two cars away. Fortunately, the SUV was already empty, but the lights were still on, which meant that he hadn't been here long. My estimation of how long it would be until he returned was about fifteen minutes.

"Thanks for driving," I told Kendrick, with my eye on the SUV in case there was any movement.

"Well, I couldn't let you drive since he would recognize your car," Kendrick explained. "That aquamarine Prius is great for finding your car in the grocery store parking lot, but horrible for spying. It's too recognizable to be stealthy."

Without breaking my focus, I responded, "Not all of us got a practically brand-new Volvo passed down to us by our fathers as a college graduation gift."

"Your parents helped you with the down payment for your Prius," he replied accurately. "They would have helped you buy any reasonably priced hybrid you chose. Gives you one less excuse to visit them if you get good gas economy." If I parked in a private garage, I would have looked into a plug-in hybrid option to use even less gas than I did now. Not that either of us drove much anyway with how close we lived to the office. Outside this section of downtown Kansas City, the public transportation system was ripe for growth and improvement. Our cars would be a necessity once we transitioned from apartments to houses in the suburbs.

The chirp of a car being unlocked with the remote accompanied by the flash of lights could be seen a few seconds before I saw Sullivan's familiar figure climb into the driver's side of his vehicle. He waited about thirty seconds before starting his car and reversing from his spot. Kendrick waited a few seconds more before doing the same, keeping enough distance between us and Sullivan that he wouldn't be able to recognize our faces. We hadn't followed him very far before he pulled into a parking lot off Baltimore Avenue. Rather than directly following him, Kendrick took a lap around the block.

"What if we miss him?" I asked worriedly. I could see his logic in this approach, but my mind was swarmed with worst-case scenarios.

Instead of answering, Kendrick continued with his plan. When we passed the parking lot again, we could see Sullivan walking east on 14th Street toward Main Street. We stopped by a red light at the intersection, long enough to watch Sullivan as he crossed two streets and entered the front doors of Blue Sushi. "How does sushi sound to you?" Kendrick asked, choosing to park in the lot on Truman and Main.

"It would have been cheaper to walk and take the streetcar here," I said, not as an insult to Kendrick, but more as a jab at Sullivan.

"Maybe he wants his car nearby when he's done," Kendrick tried, "but that doesn't make sense. Two Light is next door to us. Let's go see who he's with before we jump to conclusions about this."

“It’ll look weird if we wear our sunglasses inside,” I said with disappointment.

Kendrick shrugged and opened his door to get out. There were so many cars around and people on the street that it wouldn’t have mattered whether we had our sunglasses on or not unless he was specifically looking at us. When Kendrick told the hostess we would need a table for two, I couldn’t help but think that under different circumstances, this would feel like a date. Even under these circumstances, it was hard not to feel that way.

Blue Sushi was just starting to see the Friday night dinner rush, and it appeared we had shown up just in time. I wasn’t sure how we would find Sullivan in all this busyness, especially with outdoor seating options. The whole ordeal was beginning to seem hopeless.

“I’m going to the restroom,” Kendrick said after we had ordered our entrees. “If I can even find it in this madness.”

I utilized the time alone to observe my surroundings. Nowadays, people were often distracted and occupied by their smartphones. They hardly registered that I was watching and analyzing, aware of the shifting dynamics in the room. There was no sign of Kendrick in my immediate surroundings.

Kendrick seemed flushed when he returned to our table, the opposite of what one should be after going to the restroom. “I got it,” he smiled triumphantly, and it took me a moment to realize what he meant by those three small words.

“How?” I should have known he would never let me down.

"I saw him on the way to the restrooms," Kendrick said. "I really did need to go, but I also knew it would give me the perfect excuse to walk through other parts of the restaurant. He's sitting at a table with the same girl I saw him with on the streetcar. He was so oblivious that I got photos of their kissing without his noticing someone was watching." He pulled his phone from his pocket and swiped through his snapped photos. The first showed Sullivan's face in full view; there was no mistaking that it was him. There were a few of the couple as they kissed, the very evidence we had come here for.

"Too bad we already ordered," I said, leaning back in my chair.

"Too bad? This was as good an excuse as any to get sushi." Leave it to Kendrick to take advantage of the situation. No guy would see a disadvantage in a mission involving delicious food. Many of my friends had recommended this place, but it hadn't moved from my list of suggestions until now. I couldn't shake the feeling that this closely resembled a date, which made me nervous.

The waitress brought over our orders: shrimp tempura maki for me and white tuna sashimi for Kendrick. It was no exaggeration to describe his expression at his food as "a kid on Christmas morning." Despite the hunger that he had successfully kept hidden, he insisted on using chopsticks to eat his food because it offered a "more authentic experience." Due to how they slowed down the rate of eating, chopsticks might have been better for digestion anyway. I decided to use chopsticks for everything but my rice. As far as I knew, sticky rice was the only type suited for chopsticks.

After the empty plates were cleared and the bill was paid (Kendrick insisted on covering my meal), we were standing at the pedestrian crosswalk, waiting for our turn to cross the busy intersection. Kendrick's posture straightened and stilled at the same moment that I heard the raucous voice of Sullivan O'Hare echoing above the mull of noise and heading in our direction. The light wouldn't change fast enough, and he would recognize my face if he got too close. My mind went into full panic mode as various escape plans flashed through my mind, all of which would make us seem even more suspicious. Kendrick, however, seemed to thrive under stress, and I could see the lightbulb moment when it hit him.

Faster than I could process, he pulled me close to him, his lips on mine in a kiss. I had to fight to keep my knees from giving out at both the shock and serendipity of the moment. It wasn't just a kiss meant to hide our faces from the confirmed cheater, but something much more. I could feel it in the way his lips moved, gentle, yet teasing and longing. My mind buzzed and butterflies erupted in my stomach. Kendrick's hands were on the small of my back, holding me close enough that I could feel his racing heartbeat. This unexpected moment was greater than everything I had imagined and dreamed it would be. Before the surprise could wear off, my lips were full participants in the very public display of affection and diversion. The sensation of sparks was overwhelming, erasing our surroundings from my mind. His lips were believable; in any other circumstance, I would think this was a kiss from years of pent-up feelings.

"Get a room!" I could faintly hear Sullivan say as he moved past us with his date to cross the intersection. How ironic of him.

Once he was certain that Sullivan was on the other side of the road, Kendrick broke the kiss, resting his forehead against mine. Our breathing was in sync, and our heart rates slowed down to a normal pace as we waited for the pedestrian crossing light to change again. We were frozen that way until it was our turn to walk, neither of us saying anything to the other. Without making eye contact, we found his car, took off our wigs, and drove back to the apartment building. I refused to think about or process what had happened until I was alone.

When I checked my phone after showering, Kendrick had sent all his photos, leaving it in my hands to break the news to my sister. That would be a conversation better had in person. There was no mention of the kiss, only a reminder of what time he wanted to get groceries tomorrow.

CHAPTER SIX

"Popcorn," I reminded Kendrick as we passed the aisle that displayed the various chips, nuts, and popcorn. As long as we were both pretending that everything was normal between us, it felt mostly normal. I shut off that part of my brain to avoid any slip-ups that my tongue might cause. My mouth seemed to have a mind of its own as of late, but I found that as long as I didn't think about something, I wouldn't accidentally say it out loud. It was getting tricky with all the secrets I had been harboring.

Kendrick threw two boxes of popcorn into the cart. "If I'm going to be sharing my snacks with you, then I'm buying twice as much," he said with a smirk. I rolled my eyes and checked the list on my phone for the next set of items that I needed. By the time I had pushed the cart to my next item, he had wandered into the baking aisle and returned with two boxes of brownie mix.

"You might want to grab some oil if you plan on making both of these," I said, knowing that he likely didn't have enough in his apartment to follow the simple recipe on the box. Without arguing, he followed my suggestion, meeting me in the dairy section with a bottle of vegetable oil and a bag of peanut butter chips.

"Before you get any bright ideas," Kendrick said, "these are all rewards for going to the gym with me." So, he hadn't forgotten like I had hoped.

One month ago, Kendrick and I had a discussion that most females didn't want to have with their guy best friend. It had started with my complaining about something that I wasn't strong enough to open or move. He helped me, but not without commenting on how I didn't do more than walking to and from work to keep up my fitness. I wouldn't be able to gain muscle or strengthen my bone density without a consistent workout that included weights, resistance, and plyometrics. Many of the technical terms went in one ear and out the other, but he wouldn't let me shy away from the conversation unless I agreed to go to the gym with him for one month and see how I felt afterward. I used my trip to Ireland as an excuse not to begin right then, and he agreed that it could wait until after my vacation. Now it was after my vacation.

I eyed my share of the groceries in the cart and made an executive decision—working out more meant that I would need more protein in my diet. I searched for a container of chicken that was closer to two pounds rather than reaching for the lightest one. I also circled back to the frozen section and bought a bag of organic strawberries to throw in a shake with flaxseed, chia seeds, and Greek yogurt. This grocery trip was more expensive than I had anticipated due to the extra items, but I knew my body would thank me for it in a week and beyond. At least, I hoped that ended up being the case.

Per our typical routine, Kendrick helped me carry my groceries to my apartment and I did the same in return. Anytime someone asked us why we didn't utilize the Cosentino's Downtown Market connected to the apartment garage, I reminded them that a superstore such as Target also carried important toiletries. The market had been convenient though on the occasion when one of us forgot to grab something during the usual Target trip.

"Do you have enough workout clothes to last you through a whole week?" he asked, bringing up the one aspect I hadn't thought through.

"Maybe this is a sign that we should hold off for another week," I said, a little too hopefully. Kendrick wasn't one to allow too much procrastination when health was the goal.

"I'm giving you half an hour to go put your groceries away, and then we are going out to get you proper workout clothes and shoes," he directed at me with his serious tone. "And I know you can afford it because you've always been good with handling your money. Plus, I have coupons, so that will help with the price. Thirty. Minutes."

I had only seen Kendrick in this mood a handful of times, and one of them was when a guy wouldn't leave one of his sisters alone after she had rejected him. There was no getting out of this. At least in this instance, he was being stern that I take my health seriously. I rushed back to my apartment to put away my groceries and take stock of my workout clothes. I knew enough about strength training to know that my Nike running shoes wouldn't be an equal substitute for the exercises that Kendrick had in store over the next thirty days. My three pairs of yoga pants were all from the loungewear line of the brand, not made for actual strenuous activity unless you counted cleaning. My wardrobe only held one moisture-licking shirt. This was going to be an expensive experiment. I would need this to become a long-term habit to make it worth the investment.

"Did you make a list?" Kendrick asked when he showed up at my apartment door five minutes later. Was I that predictable with my lists, or was this just another example of how well he knew me?

"Wouldn't you rather go shopping with a girl who knows exactly what she needs rather than one who will wander all day wasting your time and energy?" I asked in return, meaning it as a rhetorical question to which I already knew his response.

When Kendrick got his driver's license in high school, one of the stipulations tied to borrowing his parents' car was taking the oldest of his younger sisters to the mall on several occasions. They knew, or at least trusted, that Kendrick was protective enough of his sister Katrina that he would not only keep her away from other teenage boys in the area but also that he wouldn't abandon her to meet up with his date. Their logic meant that once every two months, Kendrick spent his Saturday afternoon following Katrina from store to store where she would often try on clothes she couldn't afford. When I wasn't busy with homework, I kept him company in those various stores, many of which had gradually been bought out by other brands or closed due to bankruptcy. While all the waiting was torturous for a teenage boy who had just gotten his license, she usually ended their time at the mall with one of his favorite stores or treated him to ice cream for taking her out.

Just as I had assumed, Kendrick drove toward the Country Club Plaza, the location of the nearest Nike store. We passed the Cheesecake Factory on the way to the parking garage. "Cheesecake sounds delicious right about now," I hinted.

"Cheesecake always sounds good until you look at the calorie count of one slice," he said to burst my bubble. "But maybe we can go there at the end of your first month of fitness." That suggestion was about as good as a promise when it came to Kendrick. My mouth was prematurely watering at the thought. I took the chance and looked up the nutrition facts for their cheesecake and gasped.

"Why did no one tell me that I've been eating 1000-calorie desserts every time I'm there?" I exclaimed in surprise.

"The information has always been there," Kendrick answered while he parked, "but you never bothered to search for it before now." Though I knew he only meant that statement about food, specifically from restaurants, I knew it held truth for other areas of life. For example, my gut feelings about Sullivan had always been there, and whether he had been cheating on my sister this whole time or not, he likely had been giving himself the option for as long as I'd known him.

Though I had never been an avid subscriber to going to the gym, I played high school sports, which gave Nike stores—any sporting goods store—a sense of familiarity. I could appreciate the orderly way that the orange boxes marked with the iconic swish were organized and stacked clearly. Kendrick seemed to know the layout of the store like the back of his hand. I should ask him how many pairs of Nikes he owns.

"How many pairs of Nikes do you own?" I went ahead and blurted out. He had no reason to hide the true number from me, even if I couldn't see them all at the moment to ask for proof.

"I have a pair for running, a pair for regular strength training, and a pair for high-impact strength training," Kendrick shrugged as he led me toward the women's shoe section. "Oh, and a pair or two just for regular wear so that I'm not wearing down the others unnecessarily. Since I don't wear Converse or Vans, those are essentially part of my everyday shoes. Shoe size 8, right?"

"Yes," I confirmed.

He paused before he said, "Sometimes Nike runs a little small, so I'll grab two different sizes of several types for you to try on. The reason they have so many options in each exercise category is due to the different ways that people put weight on their feet. Someone who puts more weight on the inside of their soles needs shoes that have more support in that area. The shoe that's best suited for your feet will feel the most comfortable, which is why I want you to try several."

He didn't hesitate to start pulling shoes off the shelf, handing me the two sizes and waiting on my evaluation once I figured out which size worked better. The benefit that trying on shoes had over other types of clothing was that it was easy to do sitting down except for when I had to walk around to get a good enough feel for the fit. He hadn't been exaggerating about the options, straying away from the ones that were above a certain price range. At least he was keeping my budget in mind as he shuffled through the pairs, somehow able to keep track of which ones were likely purchases. Once I had ruled out the first round of contestants, I tried the better ones again, paying attention to how they fit my left foot which was slightly bigger. I half expected that he would grow impatient with my indecision, but whenever I was taking my time, he was looking over the shoes in the men's clearance section.

Finding the right pair of shoes might have only been the first item on the list, but it was nice to get the hardest part out of the way before looking at the selection of yoga pants. There wasn't time to feel self-conscious as I threw the high-support sports bra at him to add to the pile of things he was carrying around for me. Yes, I wanted high-waisted leggings. When did women's pants with pockets become a selling point rather than the standard? While the coupon did help take the edge off the total cost, it was still a hard pill to swallow. I could afford it, but it wasn't how I'd prefer to spend my hard-earned paycheck. It almost seemed worth it to see the look of pride in Kendrick's eyes. I wondered if he would still be this elated had it been his credit card paying for the contents of the bags he carried for me to his car. Carrying them myself would have been its own workout considering there was enough that I would have to do a load of laundry when we got back to the apartments.

"You do realize that this was the easy part, right?" Kendrick teased as he fastened his seatbelt before checking behind us to reverse the car. "Most of your muscles are going to be sore once we start tomorrow, and you'll need to stretch them out. Swimming can help on the recovery days, and I'll try to start you off on muscle groups to spare you from being sore all over at the same time."

"So, what are we starting with tomorrow?" I asked to mentally prepare myself for the torture.

"Lower body," he said. "When I began exercising consistently, I read a book that mentioned how men tend to be stronger in their upper body and women in their lower body. Though it's important to be strong all over, I want to play to your strengths first until you get used to the routine. I can lend you the book if you'd like."

"But then you would miss out on getting to tell it all to me yourself," I said with a grin.

When we got back to the apartments, Kendrick set my bags down near the washer and dryer before heading back to his penthouse. "Tomorrow morning at 7," he said as he made his final exit for the day.

I opened the washing machine and was bombarded by the all-too-familiar smell of mildew. Again. Reagan's clothes were sour and damp once again. If I kept washing out the smell for her every time this happened, she would never learn to remember to move her things to the dryer in a timely fashion. It was a waste of water and electricity to wash the same load twice, and we shared the cost of utilities. In a way that reflected how my mother had taught me, I grabbed an empty trash bag from the kitchen and threw her damp laundry in, tightening the drawstring before I placed it in the doorway to her bedroom. Then, I ran the washer on a hot rinse cycle to rid the drum of any mold that could be hiding out of sight while I removed the tags and stickers from my new clothes. Once I was confident that it was as clean as it could be, I washed my laundry and moved it to the dryer within five minutes of the final spin cycle ending to leave the washer available.

I was in my room looking up smoothie recipes and ways to incorporate more protein into my diet when Reagan came home. I couldn't tell whether she was on the phone or had brought someone with her until I heard the familiar voice of Mikey. Part of me had known when I moved her wet laundry to a trash bag that it could cause a potential conflict and fight, but the repercussions of that hadn't fully hit until I heard her return. Mikey's presence would either escalate or de-escalate the showdown likely to happen when she noticed. At least Mikey could quickly escape to his apartment upstairs if things got ugly.

"Ariella, are you home?" she asked, a hint of annoyance in her tone. Reagan had found the trash bag, though it wasn't like I had hidden it from her. I wanted her to see what I've had to clean up more times than I could count. I had told her multiple times in the past that she needed to move her things to the dryer within twelve hours of washing them, and I had grown tired of being ignored about something that also affected me.

I took a deep breath, closed my laptop, and walked into the apartment hallway. Mikey had a smug expression on his face as if he wished he could have been the one to enact this type of reaction from her. "Oh, hey Mikey, I didn't know you were coming over," I said to him in greeting. Reagan was fuming as she carefully sifted through her clothes in the bag.

"What happened to my clothes?" she demanded in a way that stirred up the anger in me.

"That smell is mildew, and it's what can happen to fabric that is wet for over twelve hours, especially more than a day," I said, using facts to keep my frustration at bay. "At least fifty percent of the time that I have to do laundry, your clothes or towels or sheets are sitting in the washing machine smelling like that. Normally, I would wash your things again and then move them to the dryer just so I can start on my laundry and then remind you that you need to stop leaving your things in the washer. Then the cycle repeats itself—pun not intended. This is my way of saying I'm done because when I'm having to rewash your stuff, I'm basically doing all the work for you. Plus, it's adding more water and electricity to our utilities bill every month. That sour smell is just the consequence of forgetting. The washer is open if you want to deal with that, but you'll have to wait until my clothes are done in the dryer."

"Reagan, I'm going to go," Mikey said, sensing the tension in the air, "but you should know that Ariella is right. She shouldn't have to rewash your laundry for you, and that's what she was doing every time you forgot about your responsibility. We can hang out and work on that stuff some other time since you have laundry to take care of." I wanted to hug Mikey for backing me up on this, but I sensed that wouldn't ease the current situation. He waved at both of us before letting himself out.

I wasn't sure what to make of her silence since Reagan's brand of anger was unpredictable. Some grew very loud while others grew very silent; Reagan could go either way depending on what the situation warranted. When she finally did speak, she sounded more annoyed than angry,

"Why did this have to happen in front of Mikey? Any other time would have been a lot less embarrassing."

I wasn't sure if she wanted an answer to that question, but as her roommate and her friend who had recently gotten information from Mikey about his opinion of Reagan, I felt that I should tell her the truth about some things. Again. "Given the way you've purposely portrayed yourself around him, I don't think he's that surprised by this."

"I know, but I would like to change that," she said. "I know you didn't intend for this to happen in front of Mikey, but I'm still mad at you and the whole situation."

"You really like him, don't you?" I asked, but I didn't need the answer. It was written all over her face.

"I would say as much as you like Kendrick, but I don't think anyone can compete with the way you feel about him," she responded to lighten the mood. "What do you have in the dryer right now anyway? I thought you finished all your laundry the other night."

My answer was another thing that might help lighten her mood. "Last month I had agreed to start working out with Kendrick—just for a month—once I got back from Ireland," I explained. "I thought he would forget and that would be that, but he brought it up today while we were grocery shopping. We start tomorrow morning, and I didn't have enough workout clothes or the right shoes. He took me to the Nike store and forced me to spend a small fortune on brand-name yoga pants and shoes that shouldn't be worn for everyday activities." Reagan didn't laugh at the short story, but she did smile.

"You'll be fine," she assured me. "Didn't you have to do conditioning at the beginning of every volleyball and softball season in high school? It'll feel similar to that but focused more on overall strength rather than the skill set needed for that specific sport. You're just out of practice."

Hearing that helped me place where the sense of dread had been coming from and why it was so familiar. Volleyball conditioning, specifically the first week, was always brutal, no matter how active I had been over the summer with various softball leagues. I could still remember the days that I would limp because my muscles were so sore from hundreds of squats, lunges, and calf raises. Sophomore year of high school, it was bad enough that Kendrick carried me around piggyback style whenever he could. I didn't think Li Jun would be too thrilled if Kendrick carried me into work that way.

What made this different was that I would have more control over how far I pushed myself in a way that I didn't in a school gym with dozens of teenage girls all trying to keep up with the coach's instructions. Kendrick could never make me run suicides. If Reagan, after being humiliated in front of her crush, didn't blink an eye at the idea of my working out with Kendrick, then the idea must have only seemed ludicrous to me.

"Thanks for that," I said to my roommate with a smile. "I feel better about it now. It can't be any worse than conditioning was."

"No problem. You needed someone to be straight with you the way you were with me today. It would have been just as embarrassing if I had come home with Mikey to move my stuff to the dryer and discovered that it was sitting in the washer smelling like that. And I know I haven't exactly been the most courteous when it comes to cleaning up after myself. As much as I hate to admit it, graduating from college felt like the end of any bit of childhood I had left, and I hadn't felt ready to grow up and be the full adult that everyone else expects me to be. Running away from that doesn't change the fact that I am an adult who needs to be responsible in everything, not just paying bills on time."

I felt relieved that she wasn't overly angry with the way I handled the situation. This was a step in the right direction for her, and even the current Reagan who had decided to make changes was different from the one who showed up to college freshman year. During that first semester away from home, she almost went off the deep end in an attempt to live out her newfound freedom. It wasn't until she failed one of her classes that she cut back on her late-night exploits to wake up on time to go to her lectures.

Reagan wasn't the only freshman who struggled with the adjustment of being responsible without having a parent to keep her accountable. Many of us had to learn the hard way that the freedom and independence to do what we wanted didn't exist without responsibility and expectations. Choices always have consequences. Just because you could do something didn't mean it was without a negative outcome.

"You know that I call you out because I care about you, right?" I asked to remind her of my intentions.

"Oh, I know," she said. "If you didn't care, you would let me spiral out of control and ruin my life or any chance that I might have with Mikey. I have to take myself seriously if I want to convince him that I'm more than just the fun girl. It's time to let my guard down a bit."

As much as I had wanted and tried to keep Mikey's intentions confidential, I still blurted, "That's the main thing that's kept him from making a move."

"Well, as much as I've needed to make these changes for myself, it's nice to know that there will be some additional benefits," she admitted and smiled to herself, the type of contagious grin that couldn't be held back. "You'd tell me if the idea of me and Mikey dating made you uncomfortable, right?"

"Reagan, I'd be the first in line to play matchmaker for you two." It was a truth I had no desire to hold in.

CHAPTER SEVEN

"Remember, proper form is more important than speed, and if something is too heavy, go to a lighter weight or do the exercise without weights and work your way up," Kendrick said to me as a reminder from his lecture on the way to the gym. "We want to avoid overtraining and injuries as much as possible."

Not only did our apartment complex have a fitness center, but our amenities also included complimentary fitness memberships at the nearby OneLife Fitness location. This morning, we stayed at the apartment complex since, according to Kendrick, it was less likely to be busy here on a Sunday morning at seven. His assumption bought us a nearly empty room to kick off our training.

It was a pleasant surprise how many exercises were simple due to muscle memory. Kendrick didn't have to explain all the technicalities with proper form when doing squats or lunges because I had done more than I could ever count during high school volleyball and fast-pitch softball. When I had imagined this moment in my head while trying to fall asleep last night, I'd assumed that once I was set and knew what to do, Kendrick would wander off somewhere else in the gym to do his workout. Instead, he did all the moves and reps beside me with increased intensity by adding weights. Though it pushed me physically and would likely result in sore muscles over the next few days, it was rewarding. My least favorite parts of volleyball conditioning had been running before and after all the other exercises, but without that, I didn't mind all squats and lunges, though I minded more when Kendrick added the jumps.

"How do you feel about incorporating kickboxing into the schedule about once a week?" Kendrick asked as we left the fitness center. "I think you'd enjoy it, and it's a great way to work your muscles and your mind simultaneously."

I pictured it in my head before I said, "I think it sounds empowering. I've always viewed people who do kickboxing as strong and able to protect themselves. It's not that I don't feel strong while doing a leg burnout, but even punching and kicking the air has a sense of prowess to it." Kickboxing was only one of many options I could incorporate into my exercise routine. It might be time to look into the dance classes I had said I wanted to try. Spin classes also appeared like a great thing to try, even if it was only a few times. The possibilities seemed endless now that I'd survived this first day.

One peek at my best friend's demeanor was enough to know that this meant a lot to him. He hadn't looked this blissful since the day after the Kansas City Chiefs won their first

Super Bowl in fifty years. It must have been satisfying to know that the team you were rooting for was the team that had won, and today, Team Fitness had won. I felt like a winner in desperate need of a nutritious breakfast and a fresh change of clothes. I checked the time on my watch, which sparked some concern for Kendrick. "Aren't you going to be late for soundcheck?" I asked with full knowledge of his usual Sunday morning schedule.

In a world where going to church on a Sunday morning was often reserved for special holidays if at all, Kendrick and I were part of the minority that had committed to go every Sunday. Mikey and Reagan normally went as well when Reagan wasn't required to pick up a Sunday lunch shift. None of us knew where Mikey was when he didn't show up, but if Kendrick asked him, neither of them ever talked about it in front of me. Kendrick was one of the drummers on the church worship team and had to be there an hour early for sound checks on Sunday mornings. Given that it was nearly eight and he hadn't even showered yet, he was likely running late.

"No, they want the other drummer to get more experience so that we can rotate more often, so I get this Sunday off from rhythm duties," he said excitedly. "Which means the four of us can all ride there together. Mikey asked me last night if he and Reagan could hitch a ride with me." All four of us leaving the apartment building together would mean that we would either get there late or that Reagan would rush to get ready on time after hitting snooze on her alarm for an hour. When throwing Mikey into that equation, the odds were greater for the Sunday morning rush scenario.

"What time should I tell Reagan that we're leaving?" I asked, confident he would comprehend how to answer.

"Tell her 9:15 so that we can leave by 9:25," he replied. He had made that mistake once during our freshman year at college and anytime he had given a ride to Reagan after that day, he always told her at least ten minutes earlier than the actual departure time. We all did. Her own family had been doing it for most of her life, and she had either never caught on or didn't mind it. If I were to take a guess, I would assume that she knew and had no problem since the motive behind it was to arrive on time.

To add to the surprises today, Reagan was awake and eating breakfast in the kitchen when I walked in to grab a banana. Confused, I checked the time on my watch to make sure it wasn't later than I had thought. Eight o'clock on the dot, half an hour earlier than Reagan was routinely up and going.

"I know I'm not the best about getting up on time in the morning," she explained, "but I'm going to have to break myself of that habit if I'm going to get a job as a teacher. And I will get a teaching job because I don't think I can take another year of relying on tips as my main source of income. As much as waitressing can be good money, it's too inconsistent. I have a few job interviews lined up over the coming weeks since schools are hiring for the coming school year."

This was the Reagan I'd been waiting to see, the one who was fearless in pursuing her passion and achieving her potential. This version of Reagan might have been able to handle the actual time we were planning to leave, but today was not the day to test that out. To keep myself from unintentionally telling her, I took a large bite of my banana and escaped to my bedroom to change and freshen up.

Perhaps it was merely a coincidence that I hadn't been able to keep my thoughts to myself lately. So far, it had only happened around people whom I was comfortable with. My lack of filter might have been evidence of fewer emotional walls. Though that seemed like the more logical explanation, the nagging feeling persisted that there was something more happening. The Blarney Stone was just a myth—a legend—but what if I had somehow become the exception, the one for whom the power would manifest? Someone who didn't normally speak up for herself would be the ideal target for the Gift of Gab. It would take some research online to confirm, but there didn't seem to be a way to reverse this gift if that was even what had occurred.

I had never had reason to believe in magic, but I did believe in the supernatural, the realm of spiritual things. I would argue that one couldn't truly believe in God—in all that He said He is—and not believe in the spiritual realm and things we couldn't see in the natural. The concept of the Blarney Stone and where it fell in the gray area between magic and the supernatural served as a distraction to my train of thought as I fought to pay attention to the pastor's sermon. He was preaching on a topic I'd heard numerous times before, but in a way that was hitting differently in light of my current circumstances.

"God spoke all that we see into existence using His word. He then created mankind in His image and gave us authority over creation. Your words and the words you choose to listen to have the power to create and change situations, even to the point of life and death," I heard his voice through the sound system.

He proceeded with a story about someone he knew who had been given a death sentence when his doctor diagnosed him with cancer. Most people would have taken the doctor's diagnosis and planned as if that word were true and final, but that man found an expert in another city to give him a second opinion. The second doctor gave the same diagnosis but knew that the cancer wasn't yet terminal if the man was willing to take some risks and be aggressive in his treatments. The second doctor was confident that death wasn't the only available option and told the man as much. If he hadn't insisted on seeking a second opinion and believed in only the first, he wouldn't be three years into remission now. That was the difference that what you speak and believe could make in your life. Just the prospect of hope and a plan to reach a different outcome had superseded what would have been a death sentence.

Here I was, trying to ascertain why my mouth was suddenly speaking as if it had a mind of its own. I didn't quite have proof though since Ireland was less than two weeks ago. More time would be required to confirm the Blarney Stone theory. What would I even do if that were true? If I told Kathleen, she would think that I was making it up, and that wouldn't help my case when I broke the news to her about Sullivan. She wouldn't be back in town until Wednesday anyway. I was undecided about telling Kendrick due to the feelings I had yet to tell him about. That could potentially open a can of worms. Reagan had too many big decisions to make right now to handle this, and there was no way I could tell her without her wanting to do what she could to help.

Mikey. Mikey was a possibility since he would have nothing to gain by knowing. He might be willing to help me test it out. He had nothing to gain by anything I might spill to him except maybe things about Reagan, but he didn't seem like the type to want dirt on someone else. I wouldn't be able to tell him anything he wasn't already aware of when it came to her anyway. Not after yesterday's fiasco.

We were in the sanctuary talking to some friends after the service when Kendrick and Mikey's aunt Jolene, the youngest of their parents' siblings, emphatically insisted that we join her and her husband for lunch at Extra Virgin in the Crossroads. My experience with Jolene had been limited since she lived here in Kansas City while Kendrick and I were in high school, but she occasionally dropped by campus to take us out for lunch during our college stage of life. To this day, I still didn't quite understand what she did for a living. It was also a mystery how she had acquired as much money as she had for someone in her early forties, but it didn't stop me from letting her treat us to free food when she offered. It might have been due to proximity, but Kendrick also might have been her favorite nephew, the common disagreement between Kendrick and Mikey. Kendrick looked at all of us to see if there were any objections before accepting his aunt's generous offer.

The four of us managed to escape to the parking lot—escape being an accurate assessment as anyone who regularly attends a friendly church has first-hand knowledge of the long journey to leave. Kendrick's Volvo followed Jolene's Porsche from the church parking lot to the parking across 19th Street from the restaurant. The nearest streetcar stop on the west side was right by the restaurant, giving riders easy access should they choose to park elsewhere. I made a mental note to remember this as a lunch place on any day but Sundays because no one thought to check to see if they would be open. I did a quick Google search for their hours and showed the group that we would need to come up with a plan B.

My routine on Sunday afternoons frequently involved making my lunch at home before taking a nap or cleaning around the apartment, making this an unfamiliar problem to me. There weren't many restaurants in the Crossroads open on Sundays, and the ones that did were typically open for dinner hours, but not for lunch.

"Harvey's at Union Station is open until 3 and has a Sunday brunch buffet," Mikey read from his phone. "It's not Mediterranean food, but it's open. We could either drive or take the streetcar there."

"You're crazy if you think I'm leaving my Porsche here when I can easily find parking at Union Station," Jolene said, and I couldn't blame her. I would be particular about where I parked as well if I had a car worth that much. Besides, driving would be faster, and at this point, I would settle for a Subway sandwich if it meant no longer feeling hungry. The workout from this morning could be partially to blame for my ravenous appetite. I was borderline hangry.

"I just want food as soon as possible, which means no streetcar that will stop," I said, being the first to walk back to Kendrick's car.

The others followed my lead, but it wasn't until we were in the car leaving the parking lot that Kendrick said, "By the way, the next stop heading south from here is Union Station, so there wouldn't have been any stops to deal with on the way." Though he couldn't see me with his eyes on the road, I stared daggers at him from the backseat. The hangry was beginning to take over.

"Kendrick, I think Ariella is hungry, likely more than usual due to the workout routine you started her on this morning," Mikey came to my defense. "It's hard for most of us to think straight once we reach a certain level of hunger. Plus, I would hate to have to take the streetcar for only one stop once we're done eating. It would be a different story if we were leaving from the apartment building when making the decision." Mikey would be the perfect guy for the task I had in mind for later.

Union Station had always been a welcome destination for spontaneous adventures and a go-to sight for those visiting Kansas City. It was where both the Royals and Chiefs ended their recent victory parades and hosted their rallies after winning championships, creating a sea of blue or red depending on the sport. Kendrick had dragged me down here through the brisk winter evening the week before the Super Bowl to see all the Chiefs banners and lights adorning the monument. Even inside, cardboard cutouts of key players and lights had been put up in celebration, attracting enough crowds that rope barriers were put in place to control the lines. My best friend the super-fan bribed me to stand in the lines with him so that he could take photos with all they had to offer. If the tickets to the game hadn't been outrageously expensive, he likely would have flown to Miami to watch that Super Bowl in person. It was the first time in decades that the Chiefs had made it to the final game of the season, but it would just be the start of many in our lifetime.

Union Station at Christmastime was another kind of beauty with the lights and the giant Christmas tree, a popular destination for family photos, engagements, and weddings. More than once when I'd been hanging out with friends, we'd had to avoid being in the background behind a bride and groom. Throughout the year, they shuffled through various events and themes aimed at attracting kids and their parents, specifically at Science City. Sometimes though, the temporary exhibits were life-changing experiences such as the Auschwitz exhibition. If you had asked me, I would say that Union Station was underrated for all it had to offer the metro area.

Situated in the Grand Hall of the station, Harvey's awaited us with their various buffet stations and all the food this hungry girl had been craving for the past hour. Immediate food was much better than food that we would have had to order and wait for. After I scoured the buffet stations for anything and everything that appeared appetizing, I also ordered mini pancakes. The amount of food I had gathered appeared overwhelming until I caught sight of the multiple plates Kendrick and Mikey had somehow balanced in their hands, though not without the waitressing help of Reagan. Jolene's husband Ryan didn't have quite as much as the other boys, but I guessed that he focused more on multiple trips rather than gorging the first time through.

Jolene, who had grabbed the least from the buffet, was the one doing most of the talking since the rest of us had full mouths. Her husband couldn't seem to keep up with all her wild tales involving private jets, international meetings, and parties where caviar was an appetizer. Or he didn't show interest because he might have gone on all these excursions with her, and this was a retelling of what he already knew. None of her stories gave me any clarity about her job or what her company did that would involve so much extravagance. My best calculation would be that her job was related to commercial real estate investment and development. With how much she talked, I couldn't help but wonder if she had ever visited Ireland and kissed the Blarney Stone herself.

I was returning to our table from my second trip to the buffet when I overheard Jolene ask, "So, Mikey, how long have you and Reagan been dating?" As awkward as that question might have been, my curiosity wanted to know how they would answer.

"We're just friends, Aunt Jo," Mikey said convincingly enough that she didn't press the issue. Mikey and Reagan exchanged shy glances, something I alone observed about the two of them. It was merely just a matter of time now that Reagan was making some career changes and letting her walls down around him. She certainly wasn't going to be finding random guys to date for a week anymore with Mikey as a legitimate option. Not that she did that much these days anyway.

"What about you, Kendrick?" Jolene shifted her attention to her other nephew with an open-ended question.

"What about me?" Kendrick said to dodge disclosing anything about his personal life unless directly asked. With Jolene as his aunt, he was well-practiced at it.

I shouldn't have been surprised by her question given that she was the type of person to have the audacity to ask anything (as seen by what had just happened to Mikey and Reagan), but when she asked, "Are you and Ariella dating yet, or is that something the two of you are still dancing around?" I was taken aback. It wasn't that my family members hadn't questioned me about the very thing, but ordinarily, Kendrick wasn't around when they did. It was always, always more embarrassing when both parties were being bombarded at the same time.

I tried not to make direct eye contact with him, but from the corner of my eye, I could see the blush that tinged his cheeks and ears. "As Mikey said, just friends," he choked out before he coughed and drank several gulps of water. Jolene didn't buy it—the suspicion was evident on her face—but she decided against interrogating him further, sensing how uncomfortable we both were with the topic.

"Well, what else is going on in your lives?" she continued with her questions. "How is the penthouse apartment? I hear the view from both One Light and Two Light is stunning."

Mikey piped up first, "I don't appreciate it as much as I should, but Ariella likes to borrow our balcony. She gets more use out of it than we do most of the time."

"Smart girl," Jolene said to me with a smile. "Kendrick?"

"Just the usual," he replied with a shrug. "I work forty hours a week, go to the gym six days a week, and play drums on the worship team most Sunday mornings. Nothing noteworthy happening in my life currently, but if there's any major news, I'm sure you'll find out along with everyone else." When he summed up his day-to-day life like that, it sounded mundane. Occasionally, the life of the average adult could strike one as boring. It was the idiosyncrasies of the individual days that had helped keep it from being too rote. My recent vacation to Ireland was the spice she was in search of.

"I got back from a trip to Ireland a little over a week ago," I said. Her eyes instantly sparked at the notion of hearing another's stories of international adventures. Though Kendrick and Reagan were both already familiar with what I shared, they did a decent job pretending to be as interested as Jolene was. This was all for her anyway since she would be the one paying for the food. In all the years that I had known her, she refused to let any of us pay for our meals.

Once I had given her the highlights, she said, "Oh, I adore Ireland. I've been trying to convince my boss for years that we need to expand there, but he's been dragging his feet. He claims that Italy is still a viable market due to the high volume of tourism as if Ireland doesn't also attract tourists with the castles and such. Just you watch though, once I tell him about the popularity of Blarney Castle, he'll suddenly be all over my idea." Maybe Jolene's job was in the hotel industry since she had shown so much interest in tourism. I could never quite grasp how someone so talkative could simultaneously be so elusive. It wouldn't surprise me if she changed her accent to match whichever part of the world she was in at the time.

She handed both boys $100 bills when she hugged them goodbye in the parking lot, whispering something to each of them that I couldn't hear from where I stood by Kendrick's car. Whatever it was, she didn't intend for Reagan and me to hear, which was out of character for Jolene. While she performed her farewells, her husband had fetched the car and picked her up, seeming more like a chauffeur than a partner in a lifetime commitment. I'd speculated that the reason they were together was that his quiet stability balanced out her larger-than-life personality. It would have been the classic "opposites attract" situation.

"I love Aunt Jo, but being around her is exhausting sometimes," Mikey said as he slumped in the front passenger seat. "It's ironic how someone who carries most of the conversation can also be so draining. My dad says she had to have a big personality to stand out as the youngest in their family."

"She's great in small doses," Kendrick agreed as nicely as he could. "And you have to admit, it's nice that she's not stingy with her wealth. I've heard of other families being torn apart by wealth, but Jolene has no issue with sharing her good fortune. Given her age and lifestyle, any kids she has will likely be adopted, but unless she changes or hires a live-in nanny, I don't anticipate that happening either."

"Must be nice to be the favorite nephew then," Mikey teased Kendrick.

Kendrick rolled his eyes and said, "Weren't you paying attention in there? She asked about your love life before she asked about mine. Jolene doesn't have favorites; her favorite person is whoever she's with right in that moment because they are the only ones who can pay attention to her stories."
He had a point. I tried to imagine what she would have been like as a child before she had all her stories. She had likely

made up stories then too, or she was one of those people who constantly experienced strange situations.

When we reached the parking garage at the apartment building, Reagan dismissed herself from further socialization so she could take a nap and clean her room. We all stared at her in disbelief, but she gave us a proud smile. I followed her to our apartment to change into my swimsuit so I could meet the guys at the rooftop pool.

CHAPTER EIGHT

By some miracle, I arrived at the pool before both Kendrick and Mikey. Sunshine reflected off the light blue water of the resort-style pool, and I claimed the only three seats together that remained. One benefit of apartment buildings such as this was the lack of tenants with children. I didn't mind children, but when there was a pool around, they tended to be loud and splash and be rough. At least half of the other residents had dogs, but they cleaned up after their pets and wouldn't bring them to the pool. As a result, only adults were in the area, soaking up the warmth of summer. I pulled a book out of my beach bag to read while waiting for the slowpokes. When a shadow darkened the crisp pages, I knew I was no longer alone.

"Is that a new swimsuit?" Kendrick asked me, a question that warranted a strange look from Mikey. I glanced down for a moment at my tropical print high-waisted bikini and tried to remember how long ago I had bought it. If my memory was correct, and it usually was, this was something I bought in the early spring when I was growing tired of the cold temperatures and wanted tangible hope for warmer days.

"New enough," I said. The two cousins put their belongings down on the chairs on either side of me. Kendrick didn't hesitate before stepping into the pool. Mikey stretched out on the beach chair next to me in no rush to join his cousin.

I resumed reading until I heard Mikey say to me, "You know that it's unusual for a guy to notice if a girl's swimsuit is new, right?"

"What do you mean?" I asked, hoping for clarification rather than more cryptic observations.

"Let me rephrase that," he said and turned his head toward me though I couldn't see his eyes through his sunglasses. "Obviously, any straight guy is going to notice a girl in a swimsuit, particularly if she's attractive, which you are. They may even notice a particular color or pattern. But when a guy has taken note of a girl's swimsuit closely enough to recognize if she's wearing a specific one for the first time, it means he pays attention to her and has been long enough to decipher that. If Kendrick only saw you as a friend, he wouldn't have paid that much interest to your swimsuit collection." That was a logical argument coming from any guy, let alone a family member who lived with Kendrick.

"If Reagan had joined us in any swimsuit, you would be a complete goner," I said, and he wouldn't have been able to convince me otherwise.

Knowing what I was hinting at, Mikey responded, "That girl is a true test of my resistance. It was easier when she wasn't making changes in her life and letting me get to know her. I came close to offering my help with her cleaning, but the napping part gave me a reason to follow through on my original plan to play the third wheel instead. Though, I'm currently talking to you more than Kendrick is. Sometimes I wonder if he's too comfortable in his friendship with you to know how to make a move."

"Would you be willing to help me with something?" I asked as soon as I remembered what I'd been contemplating that morning.

"If you're going to ask me to put in a good word for you with Kendrick, you don't need my help," Mikey said slightly teasing.

"It's not that," I said. "Let me tell you the whole story." Conveniently, I had shared my adventure at Blarney Castle during lunch earlier that day, making it easier to explain my hypothesis to Mikey. His sunglasses made it impossible to read his face, to be able to discern whether or not he thought kissing the Blarney Stone was a credible enough connection to my *out-of-the-blue* inability to keep my mouth shut. I ended the spiel with my request for his help in testing it out.

Once I'd finished, he took his time thinking through it all before giving his perspective. "We're going to experiment to see if there's enough proof, as well as any limits or exceptions there might be. The Gift of Gab is too broad of a term to know how that would play out in someone's life. As for your concern about reversing the effects, you could probably stand to voice your opinion more often anyway. You're too conflict-adverse sometimes. I wouldn't worry too much until we know more."

"So, where do we start?" I said, ready for whatever he wanted to throw my way.

"Let's start easy. Why did you decide to study marketing as your emphasis area for business?"

"Originally, it wasn't. I think my emphasis area used to be enterprise or something along those lines. I don't remember ever choosing it, but I do remember when I had my advisor switch my emphasis to marketing. What helped me decide was learning what marketing was and how it applied in the real world. There's both science and creativity to it, with both knowns and unknowns. For instance, it's fairly easy figuring out who the target audience is going to be for a new brand of tampons, but even 'females ages 15-45' is a broad category. Some advertisements are made for those in their late teens and early twenties different from those in their thirties. Even then, it's not wholly predictable because some women prefer to buy the cheaper off-brand, while others are willing to pay a premium price for products they know will work or for those that are made from organic cotton and bleach-free materials. And while some parameters stay the same, other things are always shifting and changing. I'm not sure if all of that made sense, but it basically comes down to both the predictability and unpredictability of the industry and how the science ties into the advertising."

"I've never thought of it that way, but it makes sense," Mikey said, and I could tell by his tone that he was slightly impressed. "That didn't help me determine much though. Most people, even quiet people, can get very chatty when talking about a subject they're passionate about. Let's try more direct questions, maybe a few things you're less likely to want to tell a stranger. When did you first realize that you're in love with Kendrick?"

Out of habit, I inspected our immediate surroundings to ensure Kendrick was out of earshot and incapable of hearing both the spoken question and the answer that would soon be spilling out. I had to think about it before it would leave my mouth.

"There was a day during our sophomore year of high school when I'd had a bad morning after some jerk had randomly started a nasty rumor about me. Kendrick was dating a cheerleader at the time. She was nice, but she didn't exactly stop any untruthful gossip either. Every day she would try to get him to sit with her and her friends, and when he refused so he could sit with me, she would join us instead. I couldn't tell if she genuinely liked me or if she pretended to since I was Kendrick's best friend. By lunch that day, everyone had heard the rumor, and some were calling me horrible names.

"Even though she didn't believe the gossip, Kendrick's girlfriend didn't want to be seen with me and had given him an ultimatum to choose between me and her. Without hesitating, he broke up with her right there and then in front of everyone during our lunch period before sitting down next to me and telling all the onlookers that they were idiots for believing hearsay over what they knew to be true. That was when I thought I might love him. It was about more than his standing up for me and taking my side; it was also about how he stood up for what was true and what he knew to be right. Kendrick did that for others as well when he was certain of the truth."

"I wish I would have been that nice in high school," Mikey said. "It took a crisis moment the summer before college to force me to grow up and treat others better and take responsibility for my actions. Kendrick was always the golden boy of all the grandchildren though. I would have fallen for him too if I'd been the teenage girl in your shoes. Do you think you would have told me that story a month ago?"

Would I have said this a month ago? That was a good way to measure whether my words were intentional or taking on a life of their own. Still, I wasn't sure how to answer Mikey's question. If he had been a stranger, no. But on some level, I trusted him. Whether or not I would have trusted him with that tidbit of information either now or a month ago was nearly impossible to determine. But if Kendrick had asked, I would have wanted to hold back the truth of that story for self-preservation.

"This is harder to figure out than I thought it would be," I admitted to Mikey. "Part of it is because I know I can trust you with anything I tell you about Kendrick. I wouldn't be telling you anything you didn't already suspect or know."

"You make a good argument with that. Kendrick probably isn't a good topic for me to ask you about then since it's too safe. How do you feel about talking about Reagan?"

"Don't you think that would be crossing some sort of line?" Reagan was a gray area that I couldn't quite place on either side. I didn't want to talk about her behind her back, but I also knew she would want me to emphasize her better qualities.

"That line is exactly why I should ask you about it," he tried to explain. "It's a bit risky, but it's better to figure this out with a safe person, even if it's questionable content."

"I hate that you're right about this." Well, at least that was out in the open before the real inquisition began.

Before bombarding me with queries, he pulled out his phone. Initially, I'd thought he was sending a quick text, but he was tapping out what seemed like a novel, which was unusual for a guy. "I'm trying to organize my thoughts a bit. In case this is temporary, I want to get as much out of you as I can today." I could tell he was joking about the last part, but I glared at him anyway—a glare that he wouldn't be able to see due to his typing on his phone and my sunglasses blocking his view of my eyes.

"Are either of you planning on actually getting into the water sometime today?" Kendrick asked, startling the both of us. He was dripping water, the light catching the droplets that spanned his bare chest and abs in a way that sparkled. I was stunned speechless. As cheesy as the comparison was, he reminded me of Edward Cullen from the Twilight movies with the way the droplets glistened on his skin. Unlike the vampire though, Kendrick wasn't pale. His skin was already lightly tanned as if he'd made a habit of coming to the pool.

"We'll be there soon," Mikey said as he put his phone away. "I was just getting some girl advice from Ariella while Reagan isn't around." Kendrick's face flashed an understanding expression as he gave us privacy once again.

I allowed myself a few seconds to recover from the visual overload. Over ten years of knowing him and I still was caught off guard on occasion. Time had only made my best friend more attractive. "We should try to speed this up since I would like to get some time swimming," I said to Mikey when I was ready.

"What happened to Reagan during your freshman year of college?"

He had hit the bullseye with that question. I never talked about this; neither of us had ever talked about this since she turned things around. It was one of those topics that was rarely mentioned, but I could understand why Mikey would want to know. The truth wouldn't change his mind about whether he pursued a serious relationship with her, but he couldn't help but be curious about how bad it was.

"Reagan was very sheltered throughout her childhood growing up, and not sheltered in the way that parents should protect their children, but in a way that was over-the-top and excessive. They homeschooled her and didn't have cable or internet access at home. They also never talked to her seriously about drugs, alcohol, and sex apart from telling her that abstinence was the only real option. Getting a full-ride scholarship to a state college wasn't exactly the future they had in mind for their daughter, but she refused to go to any of the Bible colleges that they would approve of. If you ask her about it, she'll tell you that she threatened to run away and join the circus. Since she was a legal adult, they could no longer control her decisions, so they relented against their judgment. In hindsight, I think she knew more than they would tell her about the real world outside their family bubble. Rather than taking their word for it, she wanted to experience it for herself.

"The girl that was in the dorm room that first day and the girl living in my room a week later were two entirely different people, at least outwardly. On day one, Reagan had long blonde hair and wore a flannel with bootcut jeans. To this day, I don't know where she got the money, but she managed to get a completely different wardrobe as well as new piercings, a tattoo, and her hair dyed. If her taste of freedom had stopped there, it would have been fine. She joined a sorority and got wrapped up in all that. Don't get me wrong, some fraternities and sororities focus on academics, however, that was not the type of sorority that Reagan was a part of. I never knew how late she got back to our dorm at night, and some mornings, she wasn't there. Her grades were slipping because she wasn't studying and often missed class because she overslept or was hungover. Unlike her other friends though, she didn't have the luxury of attending college to burn mommy and daddy's money because she was on scholarship. It took her advisor a few tries before actually getting in contact with her to give her a final warning. If I hadn't gotten rid of the liquor she kept stashed, we would have failed our room inspection."

"This is the part of the story when I want to tell the character, 'Listen to the people who care about you and get your life together,'" Mikey interrupted. "But I guess most people need a little more drama before their issues are resolved. It takes a pretty big crisis for most people to change that drastically. Continue with the story, please."

"That night, she was getting ready for a party with a few of the sororities and fraternities. She had told me that after that party, she was going to back off from it for a while to get her grades back on track since her scholarship was her only true ticket to freedom, as ironic as that sounds. I didn't believe her, and I'm not sure she even believed herself as she said it, but there wasn't anything I could do to stop her. Anytime I tried to talk some sense to her, she argued that she was an adult who could make her own decisions. The only way she could learn was if she experienced the consequences of those choices. If I had known what would happen, I would have fought to get her to stay in the dorm that night, not that she would have listened to me. Mikey, you really shouldn't be hearing this next part from me. It would be better if she told you since it's her story to tell." My heart was aching as I recalled the events that led to the moment that changed her. Reagan had come so far since then, but it didn't change how horribly wrong that night had gone for her.

Mikey looked uncertain, but insisted, "Tell me. Whatever it is, I can handle it. I'll still let her tell me when she's ready, but at least I'll know what to expect."

Against what I would have normally done in this scenario, I pressed ahead with the climax of the tale. "When Reagan woke up the next morning, she was severely hungover and naked in bed with one of the frat guys, who was also naked. Neither of them could remember what happened the night before because both of them had been drinking so much, but others who were at the party helped fill in some of the gaps. All the other times that she didn't make it back to the dorm room, she had at least passed out after making it back to the sorority with the other girls. It wasn't until that last party that she lost her virginity, and she doesn't remember any of it to this day."

"Why didn't she report rape or something?" I could tell Mikey was angry, though he attempted to hide it since we were in a public place.

"Because neither of them was in the mental condition to have given consent," I said from having researched when a very broken Reagan returned to our dorm room the afternoon after the party. "Rape isn't just something that's done by a man to a woman, but women can also rape men. Everyone whom we talked to from that party that night said both of them had been heavily drinking before they stumbled into that room together. He tried everything he could think of to make things right with her, including quitting the fraternity and going to rehab. As far as I know, he's still sober. Don't get me wrong, I hate that this happened to her or that it happens to anyone, but it's one of the many possible consequences that come with drinking too much alcohol. If it hadn't happened at that party, she would have kept going to them until something like that or even worse occurred. Mikey, it could have been worse."

He took deep breaths for a minute or two, bringing himself back to a state of calm. "I've never been a fan of those college parties or underage drinking, not that I was much better in high school," he said. "That's enough for now though. So far, I'd say that you're more transparent than what's typical for you. Let's join Kendrick in the pool and reconvene on this topic another day."

Less than ten seconds later, Mikey had intentionally frightened Kendrick underwater. When I didn't join them after a few minutes, Kendrick stepped out of the pool and swooped me up in his arms bridal style to carry me to the water, pausing to take off my sunglasses and shoes and leave them at our chairs. I was too mesmerized to put up a fight, and truthfully, my legs were showing signs of soreness from the morning workout. Though I shrieked, I welcomed the cool water that enveloped me when he released me into the water.

CHAPTER NINE

"So, what's the deal with you and Kendrick?" Luca asked as he sat down across from me during lunch on Monday. It was the dreaded question I had been hearing since the second week of freshman year of high school. I had always struggled with it because part of me would forever remain hopeful that one day I could answer the way I wanted, not the way it presently was. It was also frustrating that so many people assumed something that didn't exist rather than assuming we were just friends. On top of all those other factors, why didn't any of these people ask Kendrick, the guy, the one who was supposed to make the first move? This interrogation from Luca seemed strategic given that Kendrick had a lunch meeting with an architect and client today.

Despite my feelings for Kendrick having found an opponent in my attraction to Luca, my mind focused on the facts, the straightforward information. "Kendrick and I are just really good friends," I answered in full honesty. "We've known each other since freshman year of high school."

"Wow, that's not what I was expecting to hear," Luca said sheepishly. "I mean, I can tell that the two of you are close, but I assumed you were dating. I've learned from experience how hard it is to be best friends with a girl without feelings getting in the way somehow."

I could feel the words coming before I blurted my thought this time. "How did that work out for you?"

He examined me with a small smile on his face, likely determining how much he wanted to share with me. It wasn't so long ago that I could easily choose my words like that. Now, I had to be careful with my thoughts if I wanted my words to be careful.

"I had a best friend who was a girl in middle school and high school," Luca confessed. "At first, it was completely platonic, but around our junior year, I developed stronger feelings for her. Instead of telling her as I should have, I let the fear of things changing keep me from making a move. Naturally, someone else made a move instead, and she ended up getting pregnant the summer before our senior year. I didn't know how to be a friend to her after that because I was hurt that she chose him. Then she was hurt because she expected me to be there for her through it like I had been all the other times. When she eventually confronted me about avoiding her, I told her the truth. Turns out, if I had just been honest with her sooner, she would have been dating me instead of having someone else's baby. She finished high school and ended up marrying the baby's father, but things could have been much different if I hadn't let fear get in the way."

"That must have been hard to go through," I replied, "but you can't live in the world of 'what ifs.' She was responsible for the choices that she made that led to that outcome, not you. Yeah, you could have told her sooner, but she could have told you how she felt as well instead of saying yes to someone else. Even if she agreed to go out with that other guy, she didn't have to have sex with him. If she fully felt the same way about you in return, she could have chosen differently." So far, so good. My words were making sense and helping the situation.

"I know that now," he said with his heart-melting smile. She could have spent the rest of her life waking up next to that smile. "But I wanted to share my experience with you in case there's more than just platonic emotions between you and Kendrick. You don't have to wait for him to make the first move."

"And what happens if he doesn't feel the same way?" I asked. It was the age-old question that always held me back. Happily-ever-afters required feelings to be both reciprocated and acted upon.

Luca's green eyes sparkled with a hint of flirtation. "Then, I would feel better about asking you out myself. Ariella, I think you're charming, intelligent, and beautiful though I've only known you a week. Any guy would be lucky to call you his own. My sole reason for being hesitant about pursuing you is that I can see there might be something more than friendship with you and Kendrick, and I don't want to get in the way of that. It's hard to find friendships that survive high school and college, let alone ones that have the potential to last a lifetime. I'm not a safety net or consolation prize, so I won't wait around forever, but if you take a risk sometime soon and find that it doesn't work out, I would like to get to know you better."

Hearing those things from someone as attractive as Luca was like an out-of-body experience. Guys weren't usually that forward with me about their intentions. I nodded at Luca in understanding, appreciative that he would be in my corner despite our friendship being so new. The possibility of a future where I was with Luca rather than Kendrick hadn't taken root until now, but when I tried to picture it, I could see the truth in what Luca had pointed out.

There wasn't a way to lose by taking action, only by waiting too long. Rejection would mean being free to give Luca a chance. Dating someone else would lessen any awkwardness with Kendrick that might come with confessing my feelings for him. Because Kendrick would be glad to see me happy with someone else if he didn't want me for himself in that way. Additionally, I wouldn't have to explain the whole sordid tale to Luca given that he would already know. How did he know of my feelings for Kendrick? I had always tried what I could to ensure they weren't obvious.

"Just so we're clear, I'd have to be blind not to find you attractive, but you're right about my having to explore things with Kendrick before I could move past it. Did you know how I feel about Kendrick, or did you just assume based on your own experience?" I asked.

"A little of both, I guess," he said with a shrug. "There are countless movies and books out there about people being in love with their best friend. Either the guy is in love with the girl or the girl is in love with the guy, or in the best situations, it's mutual and the whole story is about their journey to end up together. It's a cliché for a reason. Some would argue that things can't be platonic between a man and a woman who are that close, but that's another topic. Even if it weren't one of the most overused storylines, the way that you and Kendrick look at each other—yes, I mean both of you—is reason enough to suspect there's something more. I figured I would talk to you first since I hoped you would be more likely to be candid about it."

I couldn't pull my mind away from the racing thoughts of my best friend. It was as if a dam had been broken, and if I couldn't reel in my train of thought, I wouldn't be able to keep my mouth closed either. "I've been trying to come up with a way to tell him, but I want to make sure it's the right timing," I admitted to Luca.

"There are obvious wrong times to tell him such as work or in a group setting," Luca said, "but anytime that it's the two of you with little or no distractions would be a good place to start. The perfect moment doesn't exist, so if you're waiting for that, you'll be waiting forever."

"There might have been a perfect moment, but I missed the opportunity," I said. I'd fought back the thought all weekend, forcing myself to forget the events that took place on Friday night. No matter how hard I tried though, it would take lifetimes to forget the way his lips felt against mine. A kiss like that couldn't be erased by a few days of distance.

"What makes you think it was the perfect moment, and why didn't you tell him if it was?" Luca asked curiously.

Well, if I was going to talk about it with someone, it might as well be someone who was on our side. "Long story short, we were spying on my sister's boyfriend while she was out of town because Kendrick thought he had seen him kissing another girl. We put on disguises and followed him to Blue Sushi. Kendrick managed to take photos of the cheating idiot before we enjoyed a nice meal. On our way back to the car, we were stuck waiting for the pedestrian crossing sign to change when the cheater came out, so to ensure that neither of our faces could be seen, Kendrick kissed me."

Luca's eyes brightened, but then he hesitantly asked, "Was it a good kiss?" It was a fair question, all things considered. Before that moment on the Main Street sidewalk, I had often wondered what I would do if kissing Kendrick ended up more like kissing my brother. If it had been a bad kiss, I would have been planning a date with Luca rather than having this conversation about my kiss with Kendrick.

"Earth-shattering might be one way of describing it," I said as the blush took over. "Even though it was just a spur-of-the-moment way to ensure we weren't recognized, it felt like there was so much more meaning to it. Neither of us has brought it up since it happened, so I'm not sure what to do about it."

"He may not be talking about it, but he's thinking about it, assuming it was as good a kiss for him. That will help when you talk to him about it because now you can bring up the kiss and ask him how he feels about it. Ariella, there's rarely ever an easy way to make a move, whether it's someone you've known for a decade or someone you recently met, but the more you get used to putting yourself out there, the easier it becomes. Ideally, this would be the only time you have to take that type of risk."

"Are you telling Ariella that she should take the risk and ask for a raise?" Kendrick said from behind me. He sat down next to me, inviting himself into our conversation. Had he shown up even five seconds sooner, he would have caught the full context of Luca's advice.

Without missing a beat or needing a non-verbal cue, Luca replied, "If she's due for one and has been working hard, then she deserves a raise. You could even use it as a forum to ask if there are areas for improvement as well. Open communication between the employee and employer is essential for the growth of the company. Employers can only make changes if they know about them."

"And you know our bosses love you and see your dedication," Kendrick added. "I would do it for you if I could, but this is your battle to fight." I checked my watch, hoping an hour was about over to give me a legitimate excuse to leave. I would ask for a raise when I felt it was time to ask, and that hadn't happened yet. Given this newfound "power" of mine, it was bound to be soon.

"I've gotta go get some work done," I excused myself as I put my glass container in my lunch bag.

Kendrick and Luca moved on to talking about sports and who was moving to which team. It was hard enough keeping up with all the teams let alone which players were on each of them. Over the years, I had only been aware of the standouts or the players guys frequently talked about, usually quarterbacks such as Tom Brady, Eli and Peyton Manning, Brett Favre, Aaron Rodgers, and even Tony Romo. Football was one of the few topics that Kendrick and I never shared in common throughout high school or college. I would only watch the Super Bowl, and he was content to slowly teach me the rules and strategies of the game.

Enter Patrick Mahomes II. Living in Kansas City during a time when the Chiefs were positioned to win throughout the playoffs, I paid closer attention and watched more games. I sat on the couch with Kendrick and Mikey witnessing incredible comebacks that resulted in a Super Bowl win. The city was alive with energy and excitement in a way it hadn't been since the Royals had won the World Series a few years before. Though it took some time to recover after the pandemic and the chaos it wrought across the world, it couldn't take away the pride we had gained in being Chiefs fans. Watching more games had helped my familiarity with the positions and players for the Chiefs, but I'd chosen not to use my brain power for those beyond my local team. Fantasy football was a level of obsession I refused to entertain.

"So if Luca and Kendrick were to get in a fight over you, who would you choose?" Hannah asked once I sat down at my desk. Of course, she had been keeping her eye on me since the arrival of our new coworker. It wouldn't surprise me if most of the women in this office had been watching in eagerness for something interesting to occur. They had all grown weary of my and Kendrick's "stagnant friendship" long ago, but Luca added a new dimension to the mix.

"I doubt the two of them would ever fight about anything," I said to dodge her question. "We're a bit old for men to fight over a girl that neither of them has any claim on. Besides, if I were ever in a position to choose between the two of them, they would be the first to know my choice." Hannah was respectful enough of my privacy to end her questions there, and I was certain that she would tell the others to do the same.

It worked in my favor to not entertain her topic of choice because less than a minute later, Li Jun scurried through on his path to the restrooms. I assumed it was the restrooms, but he could have been headed in that direction for any number of reasons. A few minutes later, he came back through less rushed and paused to ask for updates on a few ongoing projects. Being in charge of the company had never stopped him from being hands-on in areas that piqued his interest. Before he walked away, I said to him, "When you're not busy, there's something I'd like to discuss with you."

"Let's talk in the conference room right now before I dive into markups for Kendrick," he said with a smile. I did as he instructed and followed his lead. I could still remember the first meeting we had at full capacity when the pandemic had finally wavered. Whether it was full of coworkers and clients working through aspects of a project or full of civil plans for an upcoming deadline, the conference room was one of Li Jun's favorite aspects of the office. We sat down in chairs across from each other. "You and Kendrick seem to be getting along well with Luca. I thought he would be a good fit for our company."

"Yes, it sounds like he's very sharp from what Kendrick has told me," I said. It was now or never, and I'd put myself in the ideal setting. "I wanted to talk to you about my performance and whether you see areas where I could improve as well as when I should expect a raise." Having said it out loud felt as if a huge weight had lifted.

He laughed for a moment before he explained himself. "I'm so sorry. I had meant to have a meeting with you about this, but then you went on vacation, and I forgot to schedule it with you. You're definitely due for a raise, and I'll make sure that gets taken care of this week. As for areas of improvement, I would say that you could make sure you're giving the engineers enough notice and a deadline whenever you need their input on the proposals. Sometimes we get so busy that we're likely to put things off if we're not aware of when they're due. Don't be afraid to communicate and even bug one of us if we need to work on them. Other than that, I think you're doing a fantastic job."

"Thank you, Li Jun," I said. "I should get back to work so you can focus on those markups."

"Can you go tell Kendrick to come in here so we can go over this?" he asked me as he grabbed his red pencil.

"Yes, I'll go get him," I said and hurried out the door to find my best friend who was at his desk. His forehead was wrinkled in concentration, and I had to fight the urge to iron out those wrinkles with my fingers.

"Are you just going to stand there and look over my shoulder, or are you going to tell me what you need?" he asked without breaking eye contact with his computer screen. During the day at work, Kendrick wore glasses specifically for blocking blue light. Even glasses couldn't make him look like the stereotypical nerd; instead, they gave him Clark Kent vibes.

I waited until he finally turned his head to look at me before I told him, "Li Jun wants to go over some plans with you in the conference room. I'll fill you in on the rest later."

"Based on your demeanor, I'm assuming that we have reason to celebrate," he said as he saved his work.

"Cheesecake kind of celebrating?" I asked a little too hopefully.

"Like authentic Italian pizza for dinner type of celebrating," he said before he disappeared into the conference room. With the way these things went, I probably wouldn't have had another chance to talk to Kendrick until we were on our walk out the door at the end of the day. He was sticking to his guns about cheesecake being the reward for a month of consistent workouts, but pizza was a solid compromise.

CHAPTER TEN

When we parted ways in the One Light elevator later that evening, Kendrick told me, "Meet me at the penthouse in half an hour. I promised you pizza, and you promised to fill me in on what happened."

I couldn't be certain of where he would take me, but the warm summer air was calling for shorts or a dress. I opted for white denim shorts and a light yellow blouse with sandals. Working in an office meant weeknights and weekends were the only time I could utilize my summer wardrobe. The engineers I worked with seemed to prefer the arctic blast of air conditioning. It didn't take me long to change, leaving me with an extra fifteen minutes. Rather than wait around my apartment, I headed up to the penthouse at the chance that we could potentially leave earlier.

I paused before knocking on the door, hearing the bass of music playing from the living room. If I could hear it from the hallway, there was a high probability that neither Kendrick nor Mikey would be able to hear my knocking over the speaker. I used my spare key to unlock the door and made myself at home on their living room sectional. If my stay here were to be longer than fifteen minutes, I would have ventured outside onto the patio. The TV had been left on low volume on one of the channels that broadcasted the Royals games. I'd always had a hard time watching baseball games on television when it wasn't the World Series, but the handful of times that Kendrick and I had watched the Royals play at Kauffman Stadium, I was as invested as any other true fan. Now that the Chiefs had a team of solid players and fairly consistent wins, I'd been waiting for Kendrick to suggest watching them live at Arrowhead Stadium, which was next door to Kauffman Stadium in the Truman Sports Complex.

"Hey, Mikey, can you help me—" Kendrick started to say as he walked out into the living room, initially too distracted by the two shirts he was holding to notice my presence. He was startled to see me there waiting for him, and I was taken aback by another glimpse of his shirtless physique. Although I had just seen this at the pool yesterday, my brain registered it as more intimate here in the privacy of his shared apartment rather than in a public place surrounded by the other apartment residents. The awkwardness hadn't solely been me since he had paused mid-sentence when he looked up.

Mere seconds passed, but it could have been minutes according to my sense of time—minutes of Kendrick and I staring at each other silently in the charged atmosphere before Mikey emerged from his room to check on what

Kendrick needed from him. “Oh, hey Ariella,” Mikey said with full awareness of what he had walked into. He played it off well, helping put things at ease again. “Kendrick, did you need me for something?”

Kendrick blinked first before switching gears back to his reason for coming to the living room. “Yes, but it’s not important. Ariella and I are going out for pizza to celebrate her getting a raise. It’s an open invite if you want to join us.”

“I’ve got other plans tonight, but you two have fun,” Mikey said before he went back to his room. Kendrick told me that he needed five more minutes before returning to his room to put on a shirt. A few seconds later, my phone buzzed with a text from Mikey.

MIKEY

I’m pretty sure he was going to ask for my advice on which shirt he should wear tonight. Looks like my cousin is trying to make a good impression even though he invited me to tag along.

Didn’t want to be a “third wheel” again? This isn’t a date. He would have told me if this were a date, and you wouldn’t have been invited.

Kendrick never asks me for fashion advice. One of you had better make a move soon, or I’m going to have to lock you in a room somehow. Or hang up mistletoe in random doorways of the penthouse.

If I haven’t told him by the time Christmas comes around and we’re both still single, you have my permission to trap us with mistletoe.

"You can mark today as one of the rare occasions that you were ready sooner than I was," Kendrick said, wearing the cerulean shirt he had been holding minutes before. The color helped the blue of his eyes pop like the blue of the Caribbean Sea. It wasn't until we were in the enclosed space of the elevator that I caught a whiff of his cologne. Kendrick always smelled nice, but cologne wasn't customary for him when going out with friends.

"Is that a new cologne?" I asked curiously. If he was going outside his norm to wear it, it wasn't weird for me to point it out.

"Jolene's husband gave it to me for my birthday, and I hadn't gotten a chance to try it out yet since my date was canceled that day you got back from Ireland," he said nonchalantly. "I like it, but I don't quite have the budget to spend what they do on perfume and cologne. If I mention it to them though, it'll end up in my birthday or Christmas gift."

"If only all of us had a rich aunt who insisted on spoiling her nieces and nephews," I teased him at the same time the elevator doors opened. Once we were in the parking garage, he jogged ahead of me to open the passenger side door of his car for me. Kendrick was without a doubt acting strange in ways that would be imperceptible if I weren't hyperaware of him at all times. Even with my constant awareness of him, I'd known him long enough to decipher whether his actions were typical. I distracted my mind by making guesses at where we were going based on the direction he was driving. Those mental musings did end up spoken out loud, but I did it quietly enough that he must have assumed correctly that I was talking to myself. The car turned into the back parking lot, but I knew exactly where we were. Bella Napoli in Brookside.

More than once during the pandemic when I was in a sour mood (a.k.a. PMS), Kendrick had ordered curbside from Bella Napoli and surprised me with their pizza. When I felt like splurging, I ordered premium cheese from here rather than the cheaper Kraft shredded cheese from the grocery store. On Mondays during dinner hours when dining in, they had a special deal on pizza, not that he would let me pay for my celebration dinner.

When I started learning Italian back in college, I would attempt to order my meals in Italian, and the waiter was always gracious enough to help. I'd suspected that without me, Kendrick and my other friends wouldn't have anyone besides the waiter to translate the menus for them at authentic Italian restaurants.

"It's a bummer that your family went to Ireland instead of Italy this year," Kendrick said. He was concentrating on his menu, likely trying to remember how to pronounce the names of the Italian dishes. "It would have been the perfect opportunity to truly test out your knowledge of the language."

Being in Italy surrounded by people whose first language wasn't English would be a step higher than trying to read novels in Italian or watching shows dubbed in Italian. It's one thing to hear the language and understand what was being spoken, but it was another to have been able to converse back in that language and be certain of what I was saying. I didn't know if I would ever feel fluent in a language other than my native tongue.

"Buonasera, Ariella e Kendrick!" Our waiter recognized us from the many times we had come here. "Volete iniziare ad ordinare da bere?"

"L'acqua per me," I replied.

"Water also for me," Kendrick said, choosing to order in English even though water is one of the easier words to translate. "I think we're also ready to order. Ariella?" He looked to me for confirmation. Two house salads, one four-cheese pizza, and one sausage pizza later, he ordered us both tiramisu and cappuccinos.

"You know, they have cheesecake on the dessert menu," I said to Kendrick once our waiter left to put in our dessert order.

He leaned back in his chair and looked me square in the face. "If you want cheesecake, you can pay for it yourself. Cheesecake is supposed to be your reward for completing a month of consistent workouts, so don't expect me to buy you any before then. Tiramisu is a lighter dessert with fewer calories that can easily be walked off when we're done here. It's also a more authentic Italian experience compared to cheesecake."

"Fine," I relented. "You make some solid points, plus, the cheesecake options here are very limited compared to that at the Cheesecake Factory. It's the perfect weather for an evening walk." I had always loved walking through the city and seeing all the lights and bustling life, but it was also something I'd never felt comfortable doing alone as a female. Anytime Kendrick was in the mood to go for a walk, I jumped at the opportunity. He must have been in a good mood if he was offering to indulge me this much on the same night.

No matter how often I saw the towering buildings and the iconic architecture, the city constantly left me in awe. After parking his car at the apartments, Kendrick accompanied me on a walk, protectively at my side to ward off any unwanted attention from other men on the streets. We took the streetcar to the stop at the Library District. The exterior design of the Central Library's parking garage made the site hard to miss with giant book spines of classic books in various colors—known as the Community Shelf—marking the building. The renovated space where the library now resided was formerly a bank.

"We should go to River Market one of these Saturdays," I said to Kendrick as we walked, thinking through the list of things I wanted to do during this season of life living downtown. "We still haven't gone to the *Arabia* Steamboat Museum there, and it would be a great place to get fresh local produce."

"How about this Saturday?" he asked.

"Sure," I said. If I put it off any longer, I was risking never following through with the idea. "Sounds like a date." Oh gosh. Oh gosh, oh gosh, oh gosh. I said that out loud. If I could, I would run home and hide under my covers to get far away from the embarrassment. I could have sworn that I heard his breath hitch when I blurted that last part. Fortunately, we were in the shadows between two street lights, and the darkness served to cover the blush that was overtaking my face. Unfortunately, the shadows also made it impossible for me to discern whether or not Kendrick shared the same blush.

"We should head back to the apartments," he said after a few minutes of peaceful silence. "I wouldn't want you to be too tired for tomorrow's workout. Getting adequate sleep is just as vital to your health as eating healthy and exercising regularly."

"Thanks for tonight," I said as we embarked on the streetcar that would take us back to our stop. How does anyone live life without a best friend like him? It was a question I hoped I would never be in a position to have to answer.

CHAPTER ELEVEN

I knocked on my sister's apartment door, certain she was home given the live video she had just streamed to her social media with her living room in the background. A few seconds later, Kathleen opened the door, her face showing surprise once she realized it was me. She must have been expecting someone else, my assumption being Sullivan. That meant that my time alone with her was scarce.

"Hey, baby sis, what brings you here on a Thursday evening?" she asked. Fortunately, she didn't sound annoyed at my unannounced visit.

"I wanted to talk to you about something, so I thought I'd try to catch you here," I tried to sound much more casual than I felt. "It's kind of a long story though, so maybe I should have called first."

"Nonsense," she motioned for me to come inside. When comparing the apartments themselves between One Light and Two Light, I wasn't sure why my sister would pay more to live here. The amenities made up for the price difference though, which is why when I did hang out with Kathleen, I came here rather than her coming to One Light. While One Light had a luxury rooftop pool, Two Light had an infinity-edge rooftop pool that showcased a perfect view of the city lights. My favorite thing to do here was go to the spa. Unlike my sister though, I couldn't justify the higher price tag to live like this all the time. I sat down on her couch, waiting for her to sit down with me before breaking the news. "Sullivan was supposed to be here soon, but he just told me he's running a bit late. So, is this good news about Kendrick?"

Kendrick? Did she think I'd come over here to talk about him? "Things with Kendrick are the same as they have always been," I said to her, and she gave me a disappointed smile. "I wanted to talk to you about Sullivan."

"What about me?" I heard Sullivan ask as he appeared in the living room. Neither of us had heard him come in the front door. Well, this certainly wouldn't go as planned. He pulled Kathleen into a hug and kissed her cheek.

"I should go," I stood up abruptly in hopes that I might escape before the truth escaped my mouth.

Kathleen grabbed my arm. "No, wait," she insisted. "You don't have to run off. Just tell me what you came here to tell me."

"Kat, I'm sure whatever it is that your sister wants to tell you can wait," Sullivan tried to argue with her. "I made reservations, and we don't want to be late."

My sister still wouldn't let go of her grasp on my arm. It wasn't tight, but it was firm enough to keep me from bolting. "Sullivan, we can wait five minutes. Ariella wouldn't have come here in person unless it was something important. Sis, tell me." Her intuition told her that what I had to say was paramount, but would that same intuition of hers believe me when she knew the whole story? I had evidence, yet I wanted to know whether she would take my side over his without the photos.

Sullivan must have known or at least suspected what I was about to disclose to my sister because his eyes shot daggers at me. I strengthened my resolve. "Kathleen, Sullivan is cheating on you," I said as straightforwardly as I had intended. "Kendrick has seen it more than once, and we even have proof."

The expression in Kathleen's eyes was indistinguishable. I had known her my whole life, seen her every emotion and mood etched across her face throughout the years, but I couldn't decipher her now. Like background noise to the main scene, Sullivan attempted to deny the accusations with declarations of his love and commitment to her, claiming that he could see his future with her. She stood like a statue, not addressing either of us. Finally, after what felt like a lifetime, she said to me, "Ariella, you should go."

"But Kat—" I said, desperate to get her to let me stay for whatever would happen next.

"Please, go," she started pushing me toward the door. "I'll call you tomorrow after work." She shut the door and shut me out of the situation. I wasn't sure what would happen in her apartment that evening, but I did know that the only way I would be able to stop worrying about my older sister was by being with my best friend.

Twenty minutes later, I stood outside the door to the penthouse apartment, waiting for Mikey or Kendrick to let me in rather than using my key. Much like how I could read my sister, Kendrick could decode me. He pulled me into a hug, the very form of human touch that I needed in this moment of uncertainty. I didn't have to tell him where I had come from because he was already aware of my intentions for the evening. He wouldn't force me to talk about it, and my mind was too numb to concoct words that would spill out accidentally. I didn't feel like crying because I wasn't upset or sad; I was frustrated, an anger that I often couldn't express. Unfortunately, my anger had expressed itself in tears, which is why my face was wet when Kendrick finally pulled away to make eye contact with me.

"Everything will be okay," he assured me. "In the meantime, I got some of your favorite ice cream just in case things didn't go well." What he grabbed from his freezer wasn't what I was expecting though. I'd assumed he had bought Ben and Jerry's Cookie Core Chocolate Chip Cookie, but what he handed me was a Halo Top Cookie Dough flavor. It was still delicious and had fewer calories, and I'd be happy with just about any ice cream right now. When he opened the freezer to get his own pint, I caught a glimpse of the rows of various Halo Top flavors he stashed. I had never seen him buy those in all our grocery trips together.

"Kendrick, where did all those pints of ice cream come from?" I asked him, raising my eyebrow in suspicion.

"The grocery store that's pretty much downstairs," he confessed as he dipped his spoon into a pint of peaches and cream flavor. "I couldn't decide which flavor I wanted, so I went ahead and splurged a little bit. It's summer, so I figured between the four of us, they'll get eaten fairly quickly." Mikey was almost worse than I was when it came to his sweet tooth. I'd be surprised if most of those weren't gone in a week.

"She didn't even ask to see the photo," I finally said, ready to talk about it once I had finished eating the whole pint by myself. Somehow, he had eaten his faster without getting a brain freeze. "I was in the middle of trying to tell her when he walked in. I didn't want to have to break the news to her in front of him, so I tried to leave. He seemed to suspect that I knew because he was also trying to end my conversation with her, but she insisted. Kendrick, I've always been able to tell what my sister is feeling until that moment. She kicked me out and told me she'll talk to me later, and I have no idea what she's thinking."

He waited to make sure I was done with my speech before he offered a response. "Ariella, your sister knows that you only have her best interest in mind. I doubt she would accept whatever lame excuses he tried to feed her over your word, especially since you told her that you have evidence. From what I've known of your sister over the years, she's likely had her misgivings about Sullivan herself. Imagine what you would be feeling right now if you were in her shoes and your younger sister had just outed your boyfriend as a cheater in front of him."

"I would want to handle it on my own," I said immediately without a second thought. "Of course, I would be grateful to her for telling me the truth, but it would be my mess to deal with. And I wouldn't want her around for that since the whole situation is already humiliating even though it's all due to his bad choices. I get why Kathleen didn't want me around for that, but I still would have liked to be there for her because I know this has to be hard."

"Give her time," he reassured, "she'll call you and let you know how she needs you to be there for her when she's ready. For now, you're stuck with me and maybe Mikey if he ever comes home."

Mikey had a way of hiding out in his room sometimes during weekday evenings when I came over, so I hadn't noticed the signs of his absence. Even a less extroverted Mikey would come out for food though, and he was nowhere to be seen. "Where is that cousin of yours?" I asked out loud.

"He's been acting a bit strange lately, now that you mention it," Kendrick said. "Should we do a little spying? He enabled location sharing with me on Find My Friends."

"Does that mean that Mikey could also spy on you were he to get bored enough to do so?"

"In theory, but he's never that bored," Kendrick said. "I'm not bored, but you need something to get your mind off your sister and Sullivan, so spying it is. Although, your last adventure in spying is what led us to this moment now."

He pulled his phone from his pocket to open the app while I scooted closer to him on the couch to look at the screen with him. I thought my eyes must be playing tricks on me or that

I was misreading the map. "Are you seeing what I'm seeing?" I asked Kendrick and waited for his confirmation.

"I can promise you that he's not in this apartment," Kendrick said with certainty. "His bedroom and bathroom doors are both wide open. That kid has the uncanny ability to smell out ice cream."

"You make a good point. Would he be somewhere else in the building? We do have some pretty great amenities that we don't take advantage of often enough. The pool and the fitness center are both probably options since Mikey hadn't worked out with us this morning." There was one other place though, and something in my gut was unwavering about the prospect.

Kendrick said, "I think you and I both know where Mikey is." We stood from the couch and made our way to the apartment elevator, Kendrick turning off the lights and locking the door behind me. He didn't anticipate any of us coming back up to the penthouse anytime soon. The elevator stopped on my floor. As silently as I could, I unlocked the door to my apartment, and we tiptoed inside. The sound of the dryer—Reagan's clothes drying promptly—covered any noise our feet would have made on the hardwood floor.

Though we should have been surprised by what we found in the living room, neither of us seemed to be. Given the events we had witnessed up to now, seeing Mikey and Reagan kissing on my living room couch was the more normal of the two affairs I'd had to deal with today. Kendrick and I shared a knowing look before Kendrick coughed to catch their attention. They pulled apart, and Mikey wiped her lip gloss off his mouth.

We all looked at one another in awkward silence until Kendrick decided to be the first to speak. "You know, usually people who are just friends don't make out like that," he said, likely wanting to get some explanation. I would have to remember that he said that when I finally brought up our kiss in the future. Friends don't kiss their friends the way he kissed me on that sidewalk.

Reagan looked expectantly at Mikey. He couldn't wipe the smug smile from his face even when he admitted to us, "Technically, we just got back from our first date." Now they both shared a guilty expression for not having told us about their date plans until now.

"Way to keep us in the loop," I said, and Kendrick chuckled at my reaction. "Instead we have to figure it out using location sharing. If you didn't want us to catch you, you should have chosen a location that we didn't both have a key for."

"This wasn't exactly planned or thought out well," Reagan piped up. "I was going to tell you everything tonight."

Mikey explained further, "She got an official teaching job offer this morning, so we went out to celebrate. It wasn't until we were eating dinner together that I asked her if I could pay and consider it a first date. I was simply giving her a kiss goodnight like the gentleman I am."

"Wait, you got a new job?" I asked excitedly and sat next to her on the other side of the couch. "Why wasn't I invited to the celebration dinner?"

"Because Mikey has been biding his time to ask out Reagan," Kendrick outed his cousin. As if he could sense my nagging curiosity and desire to bombard Reagan with questions not suitable for the guys to overhear, he told Mikey, "We should head upstairs and let the girls catch up. I stocked our freezer with ice cream." It lacked subtlety, but it got the job done quickly. No more than sixty seconds passed before I was free to interrogate my roommate.

Reagan was the first to start talking. "I'm sorry that I didn't tell you sooner, but things progressed so quickly that I haven't even had time to fully process it all yet. I got the call with the job offer this morning. One of the upper school English teachers at Pembroke Hill School is pregnant and due around December. I'll be her assistant starting the school year and when she goes on maternity leave, I'll be taking over the class for her. Eventually, I'll have a class of my own, hopefully, next year if it all works out, but this is a great opportunity to learn and get used to being in charge of a classroom before I reach that point. Plus, it's a great school, one of the best in the metro area."

"It's an expensive school," I said, remembering the summer during college when I was a nanny. All three of the kids attended that school during the school year, and I'd had to drop off the oldest for soccer practices. One day, I decided to take a peek at the cost of tuition for the school and was flabbergasted at how much parents must be paying to send their kids there. Some children would have attended on scholarship, but for others, their parents made big money. One year for one child was the equivalent of buying a car with cash. I would hope that their staff was paid well considering how much the tuition was.

"Yeah, one of the disadvantages will be having to teach some kids who don't understand that their family's standard of living is high compared to the average person," she said thoughtfully. "I would hope that those parents have been teaching their children about responsibility and the consequences of their choices, but I know there will be teenagers in my classes whose parents buy them brand-new cars when they turn sixteen. I'd guess a good portion of them live in those extravagant houses in Mission Hills and Brookside. But they are highly esteemed for their academics and college preparation, which means that the parents likely value a good education. I have a good feeling about this opportunity."

"Good, you should be excited," I said to reassure her. "I'm trying to make sense of how a celebration dinner turned into a make-out session."

She rolled her eyes and sighed, attempting to collect her thoughts. "Mikey was the one who called me about if I'd heard back from any of the schools. He must have crazy intuition because it was not even ten minutes after I'd gotten the offer. After I told him, he suggested going out tonight to celebrate. I didn't have much time to discuss any of the logistics since I had an afternoon shift today at the restaurant, so all we had agreed on was a time. I had incorrectly assumed that he would get in touch with you and Kendrick and invite you both to come, but by the time I realized he hadn't, it was too late. Turned out that he was looking for an excuse to take me out on a date—"

"Which you certainly had no problem going along with," I finished for her.

"And of course, I had to kiss him. I've always felt this insane chemistry whenever I'm around him, and I had to know whether or not that would translate over into a kiss." She stared off into the air as if lost in her own world for a moment. Well, those two were goners.

"Just make sure you're taking the time to get to know each other," I said as I settled on that piece of advice. "Even though we're all friends, you two don't know each other very well yet. When there's instant chemistry, it can be easy to mistake that as something more substantial than it realistically is."

I could still remember when Kathleen treated me to a girls' day out at the nail salon and spa the week before the first day of my freshman year and her senior year of high school. Over the years, I had watched the way she flitted from one crush to another with broken hearts along the way. She would cry herself to sleep at night when a boy broke up with her, but less than a month later, her obsession would be fixated on someone new. It was a constant cycle that I never quite understood. The boys were cute, yet they didn't seem worth the time and energy that my sister was willing to give them.

Throughout middle school, most of the guys in my class were still working through the awkward stages of puberty with overnight growth spurts and cracking voices. Despite the disinterest I had shown in dating during middle school, my sister had taken it upon herself to pass down some wisdom she had learned the hard way throughout her high school relationships to prepare me for the four years that would follow. To this day, Kathleen's choice of boyfriends was questionable, but she still gave sound advice, much of which I had passed on to Reagan and other friends I had throughout college. Having an older sister with experience saved me from learning most things the hard way.

"I know you're right," Reagan said as she got up to collect her clothes from the dryer that had stopped. "He and I are both hoping that if you and Kendrick couple up, we can double date as a way to keep things from progressing too quickly. Of course, we completely respect whatever you two decide in terms of your relationship and whether you want to pursue something more than friendship. That's between you and Kendrick." She disappeared into her bedroom to put away her clean laundry.

No calls or texts had come from Kathleen yet, but there was an unread message from Mikey.

MIKEY

Kendrick just told me something very interesting...

I'm going to need more information than simply saying Kendrick told you something interesting. Anything sports-related is interesting to you two.

Fair point. He told me the story about how he kissed you last week. He thinks he freaked you out and is scared to talk to you about it because he doesn't want to make it weird. It's time for you to tell him. Strike while the iron is hot as they say.

I know. I will.

How have you not accidentally spilled it considering your newfound Gift of Gab?

I've found that if I can control my thoughts, then I can control my words. As long as I'm not thinking about how in love with him I am while I'm with him, then it doesn't come out. I may not be able to reign in the gab, but I do still have full discipline over my thoughts.

Well, it's time. This week. I can keep a secret, but this unspoken thing between you has gone on too long.

This had gone on too long. Keeping it to myself in high school was one thing, and given his relationship during college, I couldn't exactly do anything about it then, but it had been years now since graduation. Kendrick and I had both been single for years. We were both financially stable adults with good jobs and little to no emotional baggage—two adults who had known each other and stuck around for all the explorative years.

I lay on my bed, emotionally drained from the day. The glass eye of my fuzzy stuffed dog was uncomfortable against the back of my head. I pulled it out to look at it—the white, green, and purple fur in desperate need of a good wash. During high school, Valentine's Day progressively became a bigger deal each year, with girls showing off whatever gift their boyfriends or secret admirers had delivered to the school office. Kathleen was among those who regularly received the most gifts, while I did my best to ignore the faux holiday altogether. Senior year, I was unexpectedly called to the front office to pick up a gift that had been delivered, a stuffed dog. The note attached simply read in plain text, "Never forget how special you are," without any signature. Though the giver never came forward, Kendrick's youngest sister recognized the stuffed animal from when Kendrick had bought it while out shopping with the family. His mom confirmed the story, but I had never confronted him about it to this day. It was now or never.

I jumped up from my bed with resolve, ready to head back up to the penthouse, when my phone rang with my ringtone assigned to Kathleen. She was more important right now.

"Hello?" I answered as I sat back on my bed, gazing through my windows at the sunset behind the downtown cityscape.

"Hey, sis," I heard my sister's voice tinted with sadness, but without any sniffles or signs of crying. "I just wanted to thank you for coming over here to tell me the truth, even though it was a hard truth. You shouldn't have been put in that position, but you did the right thing. I broke things off with Sullivan. To be honest, I've been thinking about ending things with him for a while, and your honesty is what gave me the push to finally do it."

"Are you okay?" I asked her and then added, "Wait, why didn't you break up with him sooner?"

I could hear the rumble of her ice dispenser in the background while I waited for her response. She admitted, "It was convenient having someone to drop me off and pick me up from the airport and to check on my cat while I'm gone. It's also nice having someone to pay for my dinner when we go out. Apart from the blatant cheating, he treated me well. Overall, I wasn't that attached to him, just the idea of him, as horrible as that sounds. That detachment likely inspired him to seek affection elsewhere, not that he's innocent in any way. It's all for the best. Are you up for checking on my cat while I'm away on work trips for the time being since you're already synced to my calendar?"

"Of course, you know I'm willing to help you out," I said fully relieved that my sister wasn't heartbroken over Sullivan.

"By the way, he claimed that you and Kendrick must have been following him around to have gotten proof of his indiscretion. I told him he must have been imagining things, but I wouldn't put it past you take advantage of an opportunity for spying. You were obsessed with Nancy Drew when we were younger and I doubt you've fully grown out of your inkling to solve mysteries. How did you get your evidence?"

Confident that she wouldn't be upset or angry at the tale, I shared Friday night's string of events with my sister, including the wigs and the kiss. Throughout the story, she gave her comments such as, "Sullivan really does have an obvious license plate cover," and, "he could have walked to Blue Sushi from here, so it's fishy that he would pay for parking when he could have left his car here." With Kathleen, the pun was always intended. Because the kiss was after the climax of getting the photos, it served as the twist at the end.

"About time," Kathleen said while chewing on ice. It was a bad habit we both shared, but for me, I usually only did so when stressed. "If I were you—and it's a good thing I'm not—I would march up to that penthouse right now and kiss him again. Actually, it's late, so he's probably in bed, but that's beside the point. My point is, if that doesn't show him how you feel about him, I'm not sure what else can be done. Sis, it's time to be brave again."

CHAPTER TWELVE

"I can't do any more lunges," I breathed out, the burning tightness in my legs and the acceleration of my heartbeat at war with my motivation. It had been four days since the first leg day, leaving sufficient time for my muscles to recover, but my mind was still adapting to the prospect of sore muscles more days than not. Working out was as much of a mental challenge as it was a physical one.

Kendrick finished his set of chest presses on the machine before coming to my aid. He appeared to be internally debating whether I was being a wuss or whether my body was telling me not to overextend myself. "You're probably right," he agreed with me. "Are you familiar with how to do a Romanian deadlift with proper form?"

I shook my head. Lunges and squats were common exercises for volleyball conditioning because they didn't require weights, but deadlifts without weights wouldn't have given the level of burn that our coaches wanted to inflict on us. At least, that was my theory. He grabbed a set of weights and handed them to me before grabbing a heavier set for himself. Show-off. Then, he demonstrated the exercise while verbally explaining what I needed to focus on. When it was my turn, he placed his hands on my back and waist to help me stay neutral and utilize my glutes and hamstrings. The weights and burn in my legs were the only things keeping my mind from going into overdrive from his touch. When I stood up, he was close enough that I could feel his breath.

"I think I've got it," I managed to say, breathless from his closeness since I suspected I hadn't finished enough repetitions yet for it to be the exercise. He backed away and grabbed his set of weights, counting down the set so I could concentrate on my form. Working out with Kendrick was turning out to be a good motivator despite how distracted I would get on occasion when my eyes wandered to him. I didn't have a reason to impress him as much as it was that I had enjoyed having an additional interest shared between us. Mikey was on the stair machine pretending to be focused on the sports highlights flickering across the screen. If Kendrick had also noticed the way his cousin was observing us, he was hiding it well. Maybe the guys were used to others noticing them at the gym given that they had been coming here together since we all moved into the building.

Another guy, one I hadn't recognized, sat down at the machine a few feet away from where Kendrick and I were stretching. From the moment he had walked into the fitness center, I'd had an uneasy feeling anytime he switched machines. I wouldn't describe him as sleazy, per se, but the way his eyes had raked over my body sent shivers of disgust down my spine. "Keep working out like that, sweetheart, and you'll have all the men in the building working out here in the mornings," he said and winked at me. Kendrick immediately tensed and turned toward the guy.

"She is not your sweetheart, and just because you have eyes doesn't mean you get to look at her like she's a piece of meat," Kendrick almost growled at the guy. Then, he put his hand on my lower back protectively and led me toward where Mikey was cleaning off his machine.

"Kendrick, you need to calm down," Mikey said when he witnessed the anger on his cousin's face. "He's not worth the energy." The three of us headed back to the elevator, and I could sense Kendrick slowly relaxing again. I wanted to throw my arms around him and thank him for defending me while also reassuring him that I was tough and didn't need him to protect me all the time. But, of course, Mikey was standing there with us, and we were all covered in a layer of sweat.

Once the elevator doors had shut us away from any possible eavesdropping, Kendrick ranted, "I hate it when guys like that treat women with disrespect. It's even worse when women encourage that kind of behavior from them or don't at least discourage it. All he cared about was your body when there's so much more to you than how you look. It's ridiculous that we still live in a society where women don't feel as safe as men do just because they're women."

"That would be the opposite of calming down," Mikey commented, clearly uncomfortable with the situation.

Kendrick closed his eyes as his breathing gradually slowed. He didn't show his anger often, but when he did, he needed a few moments to anchor himself again. Kickboxing might have been a healthier way for him to release his frustrations.

"I'll meet you in the lobby," I told him as the elevator stopped at my floor.

"I would feel better if I meet you at your door instead," he called out to me before the doors closed between us to take him to the top level. His response might be an overreaction to the idiot at the fitness center, but it was useless to fight him on this. It would take him anywhere from a few days to a week or two to erase the incident from his mind and go back to his usual self, the self that didn't feel the need to accompany me everywhere. On the bright side, I was almost guaranteed more opportunities for alone time with him, opportunities to confess the very things I'd held inside for too long.

As a last-minute decision, after I finished getting ready for the day, I spritzed a few sprays of my perfume that I saved for special occasions. Kendrick texted for a second time to let me know that he was waiting outside my door.

"I'm sorry if I was being overbearing again," he apologized as I locked my front door. "I know that you're capable of taking care of yourself. Sometimes I forget that you don't need me like you did in high school."

"I didn't need you in high school," I said with an eye roll. On some level though, there were instances that I did need him back then. High school had been a brutal stage of life at times, though not all of it was bad.

"Everyone needs a best friend in high school, and yours had just moved away to another state," he rebutted. "Yeah, you had your sister, but that was only for one year. Just admit that it would have been a horrible experience had we not been friends for those four years."

In an alternate reality, one in which my freshman locker neighbor was a girl I'd never met rather than Kendrick, I had imagined that she would have become my best friend instead. In that storyline, I dated more because I didn't have a best guy friend that I was secretly in love with. She and I would have sleepovers and stay up late gossiping about different boys on the football team or baseball team or basketball team depending on the week. We would both have had dates to the prom both junior and senior years with guys who were also best friends. I would have spent more nights crying over a breakup and more time agonizing over college choices. Then I would have arrived on a college campus without that best friend because she would have chosen Mizzou rather than UMKC since it was a larger college with a greater dating pool. Or if she had wanted to go to UMKC, she and I would have shared a dorm room, and I would have never met Reagan.

In that reality, Reagan might not have passed room inspections or come back after her nightmare of a first semester. Or, she would have pushed through anyway. I would have graduated college and gotten married to my college boyfriend. After a year or two of living in loft apartments downtown, we would have bought a house together in the suburbs so that we could have a yard for our dog and space for the coming baby. High school and life beyond it might not have been horrible without Kendrick's friendship, but that reality seemed so distant and foreign and out of alignment with what I had learned to want out of life. This—right here in the current moment—was the very best possible outcome because it was the only life that I could tangibly know.

"It wouldn't have been horrible," I said. "I'm sure life would have been fine had we not become friends, but it would have been different. I like things the way they are right here and now though." He found my answer satisfactory and left the topic alone. The silence between us didn't feel uncomfortable because when you knew someone well enough, you didn't need to fill every moment with conversation. While we rode the streetcar to work, he was on his phone and I watched the others riding with us. Sometimes I would imagine that this was similar to what it felt like to ride the subway in New York City but on a smaller scale.

"I have another lunch meeting with a client today, so you'll have Luca all to yourself again," he informed me without looking away from his phone. "Of course, I think it's slightly unprofessional to be having a lunch date with a coworker where the rest of the office is watching, but you can do whatever you want."

Lunch date? "Kendrick, what are you talking about?" I asked him, mentally willing him to make eye contact with me.

He put his phone away with a frustrated sigh and gave me his full attention. "Look, I probably shouldn't be telling you this, but Luca has been asking me about you since he showed up. He clearly has an interest in you, and you admitted on the first day you met him that you think he's hot. I can't tell you whether you should or shouldn't date him. Honestly, I think he's a great guy from what I know about him so far, so it wouldn't surprise me if he made a move sometime soon."

"He already did," I said and thought, but before I could get the rest of everything out, Kendrick interrupted me.

"Then give him a chance if that's what will make you happy." The streetcar doors slid open and he escaped into the sunshine toward our office building, leaving me with no time to refute his claims and accusations before the two of us reported for work.

Work dragged on the way it always did when you wished time would speed up. My ears were attuned to the pattern of Kendrick's footsteps, but he refused to look in my direction whenever he walked past. As promised, Kendrick was absent from our lunch break, leaving me alone with Luca again.

"Okay, what is going on between you and Kendrick?" Luca asked as he took the seat across from me. "At first I assumed that you had told him how you felt and it hadn't gone well, but the guy looks like he just got his heart broken. And you look confused."

"I am confused," I groaned. "He thinks that you and I are dating or about to date or something along those lines, and after he went off about it, he practically ran off and wouldn't give me any time to explain. If I hadn't had things going on with my sister last night, I would have barged into his apartment and made my confession then. My sister suggested that I just kiss him again and see how he reacts."

Luca appeared thoughtful for a moment. "That would certainly be an effective means of communicating your feelings. As a guy, my advice would be to communicate as straightforwardly and clearly as possible. There has to be a misunderstanding, or he wouldn't be acting like this. Are there any other reasons why he would be in a sour mood today?"

"There was this sleazy guy at the gym who wouldn't stop staring at me. He said something offensive to me, and Kendrick probably would have knocked the guy out if he had less self-control. He was livid for a while after."

"Offensive as in?" Luca asked for more detail.

"As in, he made a rude comment about my body," I said and rolled my eyes now that I was detached enough from the moment to look at it objectively. "That's pretty much how he acted anytime another guy has done something similar. I'm pretty sure some guys in college were scared to talk to me after they made a stupid comment in front of Kendrick. He has all younger sisters, so he's wired to be a bit protective when he suspects that a guy's intentions are less than pure."

Luca didn't hesitate before he added, "He's jealous. If you were his sister or a cousin, then overprotective would be justifiable. But Ariella, you're neither of those things nor does he look at you as those things. I don't know why you sell yourself short or keep doubting what I, and likely others, have been telling you, but whether he's aware of it or not, Kendrick is in love with you. Yes, it's scary to think about because you two have known each other for so long and have been through many seasons of life together as friends, but it's not like you're falling for people that you don't already know and trust. Look at the way he defends you; he would never intentionally hurt you. Now, I'm gonna go back to my desk and finish eating while I work because I have a deadline. Also, I think it'll ease his insecurities a bit if I'm not sitting with you when he comes back from his meeting."

I gave Luca a grateful smile as he picked up the remainder of his lunch and walked back to his cubicle. My phone screen lit up with a text from Mikey.

MIKEY

How is he? Better than this morning?

Hardly. He kinda blew up at me about something I didn't do.

I shouldn't tell you what's going on, but he seems to have chosen not to tell you himself.

Tell me what? What's going on?

His mom went to the doctor yesterday. I guess they found something that they're concerned might be cancer, so they've scheduled her to do more tests and a biopsy.

Kendrick's mom was one of the kindest, most selfless people I'd ever known. His parents—his family—meant the world to him. I quickly finished my food and stepped outside to make a phone call.

Mrs. Barlow answered on the second ring, her voice as cheery as I remembered. "Hello, dear! Aren't you at work right now?"

“I’m currently on my lunch break,” I said to her. “I heard the news and wanted to check to see if there’s anything I can do.”

“I figured as much,” she said, and I could hear her smile in the warmth of her tone. “They’re just going to run some tests to get a better idea of what’s going on. I don’t think it’ll be anything serious, but you know how Kendrick gets worried sometimes. As for what you can do, keep me in your prayers and make sure Kendrick keeps his head on straight. Maybe one of these weekends the two of you could come back for a short visit. If you suggest that, he’ll be less likely to miss work to come to see me. How was Ireland?”

“It was beautiful,” I said, suddenly longing for the peacefulness of nature there. “It was nice to get away for a bit and recharge, even though our schedules were full the entire trip.”

She laughed at my response. “Well, that’s how vacations tend to be. Even staycations are hard because you tend to want to use the time off to catch up on household chores. Anyway, I should let you go so you can get back to work. I’m very glad you called to check up on me. I miss having you around the house.”

“I miss you too,” I said. “I’ll try to plan a trip sometime soon. I’m sure my parents would love to have me home for a weekend. Bye, Mrs. Barlow.”

“Bye, Ariella,” she said before we both hung up. Kendrick was walking toward me on his way back from his meeting. Any anger he had harbored this morning had vanished from his demeanor.

"My mom?" he asked and motioned to my phone.

"Yeah."

"We'll talk about it after work," he said with a small smile. It was an improvement compared to his other moods so far today, but now he seemed defeated. I would prefer his anger over his sadness or worry, but Li Jun would be waiting for a meeting update from Kendrick.

The second half of the day went by as slowly as the first half had until I found myself knee-deep in a new marketing request. I hadn't noticed what time it was until Kendrick showed up at my desk to wait for me to save and shut down for the day.

"Did Mikey tell you?" he started by asking. At least his guesses were usually spot on when he wasn't trying to hide something from me.

I nodded, and if we weren't currently sitting on the streetcar, I would have wrapped my arms around him in a hug. "You could have told me yourself, you know," I said to him as I linked my arm through his. "Your mom is like family to me."

"She told me not to worry about it, and I've been trying to get it out of my head, but it's been simmering beneath the surface," he said, not pushing me away. "She's probably fine, yet I can't keep myself from imagining the worst-case scenario. What am I supposed to do if she has cancer and has to go through treatments?"

"Well, there's the possibility that she would have to come here to Kansas City for her treatments since we have a larger hospital system," I said in an attempt to come up with a solution that would ease his mind. "That would make it easier for you to help her. You could also visit your parent's house on the weekends. Your sisters are all old enough that they could take care of themselves for a few days, so you shouldn't have to worry about that. Kendrick, even in the worst situation, everything will be fine."

I followed him up to the penthouse, sensing that he wasn't ready to be left alone yet. The apartment wasn't empty though because Mikey was in the kitchen, the smell of bacon encircling us when the door opened. I could hear Reagan's voice as well. At least hearing her talk meant that we weren't about to walk in on another kissing session. "About time you two showed up," Mikey said, opening the oven door to check on whatever was baking in the pan.

"What's cooking?" Kendrick asked, sitting on the empty barstool next to Reagan at their kitchen island.

"Bacon-wrapped chicken," Mikey said with a proud smile. "I figured you could use a distraction to get your mind off what's going on, so I cooked dinner for the four of us. If you're down for it, I was thinking that we could also go to that karaoke bar in Westport that Ariella has been begging us to go to for months."

"Offkey!" I exclaimed. I gave Kendrick doe eyes to convince him to roll with the idea Mikey had offered. Karaoke was underrated as far as fun activities went, and it often worked out cheaper than bowling and laser tag.

Kendrick gave me a softening expression that made me confident I had gotten my way before he confirmed it vocally. "Sure, why not? Just one question though. Mikey, did you tell everyone what was going on?"

"Not everyone," Mikey smiled in confirmation. "Just Ariella and Reagan. I didn't want to have to deal with your brooding self without backup. Also, you should have been the one to tell Ariella because your mom loves her like she's part of your family, never mind the way you were acting this morning. No offense, but you're not that great at hiding your feelings." He threw his arm around his cousin in a side hug.

"And you have to forgive Mikey," Reagan came to his defense, "because you know that he would only tell us if he knew it would be better for you that we knew. And in this case, I agree with him. We're your friends, and we want to be there for you. Sometimes all we can do is help get your mind off the worry and the unknowns until there is a known. There's no benefit to imagining the outcomes when they don't help you come up with a solution."

"Fine, I can't possibly stay mad at any of you while watching you all sing karaoke," Kendrick said. "Plus, bacon covers a multitude of sins."

We hungrily consumed the chicken and baked asparagus. While Mikey and Reagan cleaned up the dishes, I rushed down to my apartment to change clothes while Kendrick did the same. We reconvened in the penthouse living room before embarking on our adventure for the night. Karaoke bars and lounges had a special place in my heart, the part of me who loved this form of taking a risk.

I flipped through the catalog of choices, finding it nearly impossible to make a decision. Mikey volunteered to go first and performed an entertaining rendition of "Never Gonna Give You Up" by Rick Astley. I could have sworn that I saw Reagan swoon while he sang a song that was directed at her.

"I think we've all been Rick-rolled," Kendrick whispered to me, and we both chuckled at his reference.

Reagan also chose an old-school song with "Bootylicious" by Destiny's Child to which Mikey said, "How did I not know that this song existed?"

"Mikey, I'm pretty sure your parents sheltered you from the many songs about butts that popped up during the 90s, as did mine," Kendrick replied to his cousin. "Except 'Baby Got Back.' That one slipped through the cracks somehow thanks to Shrek."

I figured their conversation needed some spicing up and said, "This makes me suspect that neither of you has heard of the 'Thong Song.' Don't get any ideas though. I'm not wasting my karaoke moments on a song that's best suited for the drive home. I'm still trying to narrow down my list."

"I don't know why you're not automatically going with that one," Kendrick pointed to the second song on my list. "That's your typical go-to, and it wouldn't be a complete experience without it." I had been trying to avoid doing my same-old routine tonight, but I couldn't deny his request when this whole night was meant to get his mind off things with his mom. If Mikey and Reagan weren't here with us, I would find other ways to clear his mind of the worry.

When the opening instrumental for "I Wanna Dance with Somebody" by Whitney Houston played over the speakers, all three of my friends in the audience cheered. Back in our college days, a group of our friends rented out a space for an 80s-themed New Year's Eve party that included karaoke. The week before the party, I listened to various playlists of 80s music to familiarize myself with the music from that decade and to narrow down what song I wanted to perform to ring in the new year. As the party approached, I forced myself to decide so that I would have enough time to memorize the words. I didn't need to have every lyric down, but I needed to know the flow of the song and the way the words were sung well enough to wow my peers. On a night filled with Michael Jackson, Toto, and Journey, I threw in my rendition of Whitney. That was the night that the song became an instant crowd-pleaser anytime someone was throwing an event with karaoke.

Rather than watching me like an audience, my friends joined me in singing and dancing along as strangers in the audience—who were likely drunk—applauded our fun. Kendrick was a wild card when it came to what he might choose on occasions such as this. He wasn't picky when it came to genres of music, and he had a knack for remembering songs he hadn't heard in years. His mental music library was endless.

Although I knew that I couldn't have guessed it ahead of time, I was still surprised when he sang the first verse for "Sucker" by the Jonas Brothers. In the past, he had complained whenever I played the Jonas Brothers, not because he didn't like their music, but rather because I had the tendency to play their music too much if I wasn't made aware of it. Teenage Kendrick once had to deal with a teenage me who loved their music to the point of destroying my CD from overplaying it. Now that they were back together and releasing new music, I had been taking a more moderate and mature approach. There was a small part of myself though that did an inner fangirl squeal watching Kendrick sing this song.

"Consider that my official apology for how I treated you this morning," he said once he had finished singing. "I know that I shouldn't jump to conclusions about you or your dating life. As much as it bothers me, it's not my job to protect you from any possible love interest. It would be hard if you did decide to date Luca, but I would get over it for the sake of our friendship."

"Why would it be hard?" I asked with hopes so high that I was beginning to question whether someone in the lounge was smoking a joint.

"Hey guys, it's getting late," Mikey interrupted. "I'd rather not still be here when the majority of the others here are drunk. We should head back to the apartments." The moment had been right there, so close and within grasp, but once again, it had vanished as suddenly as it had come.

There were nights that I would have preferred to stay here and watch the drunk strangers around me attempt to sing songs and entertain the masses. We would have made up stories about how they ended up here today ranging from a typical Friday night out on the town to an undercover agent for the CIA pretending to be as drunk as the surrounding crowd as a way to discreetly siphon information about an underground operation. The latter might have been a stretch of the imagination, but it was fun to picture, nonetheless. Tonight, the weariness of the day could be seen in Kendrick's eyes, a sign that Mikey was attuned to his cousin's needs now that we had all done our share of karaoke antics.

After he started the car, Mikey handed me his phone with Apple Music open, and I remembered our earlier conversation. I quickly typed in the search to find the "Thong Song" for the boys to hear. It was a powerful thing to be left in charge of car DJ duties, even if the drive back was only long enough for two songs. Mikey and Kendrick's facial expressions predicted that I would be trusted with car DJ duties more often in the future.

"Are we still on for River Market in the morning?" Kendrick asked me in the elevator.

"Wait, you guys are going to River Market tomorrow? What time?" Reagan asked excitedly.

"We're leaving here at eight," I replied to all three questions with one statement. Both Mikey and Reagan seemed to be debating whether they wanted to invite themselves along for the adventure. Wordlessly, Mikey communicated to Reagan that it was up to her whether she wanted to tag along on a Saturday morning.

She decided, "I think I'd rather sleep in on this particular Saturday. It's been a long week. Maybe we'll catch up with you guys and join you for lunch somewhere." I released the breath I hadn't realized I was holding until the relief hit.

CHAPTER THIRTEEN

With the many stops that the streetcar made along its loop in River Market, we sat and created a game plan while looking at the map.

"You need coffee if we're going to survive the day, so we should start with City Market Coffee," Kendrick said and pointed to the spot on the map. "It's right next to a bakery. The *Arabia* Steamboat Museum doesn't open until ten, so we've got some time to sit and enjoy breakfast before going."

"Why did I say that we should leave at eight if the place doesn't open until ten?" I said tiredly. "I could have slept another hour and still had time for breakfast and coffee."

"Because last night we didn't have any set plans other than the museum," Kendrick said matter-of-factly. "If we don't decide where we want to go for lunch now, you'll be too hungry to make a decision when it's time to eat lunch. And no, Betty Rae's Ice Cream doesn't count as a viable lunch option."

Sometimes, I hated how predictable I was to him. "But we can still get ice cream afterward, right?" I asked and gave an innocent smile while I batted my eyelashes.

"Fine, but only because it's Betty Rae's," he consented.

"And it's right next door to Thou Mayest, which will be perfect for our afternoon coffee," I added while comparing the map on my phone to the paper one he was holding in his hands. "No, there is no such thing as too much coffee on a Saturday. It's not like we're sitting at home consuming caffeine; we'll be walking it off. All this walking on what's supposed to be our rest day from working out."

Kendrick folded the paper map and stashed it in the front pocket of my crossbody purse. Our stop was next, and neither of us wanted to miss our stop and have to wait for the streetcar to loop back around. "Our bodies were created for movement, specifically walking," he responded after a beat. "Taking a rest day doesn't mean being lazy, but it means giving your body rest from intense training. Unless you're recovering from an injury or surgery or hiking uphill, walking is far from an intense activity."

We disembarked at the stop on 3rd and Grand, crossed the street, and walked west on 3rd Street toward the coffee shop and bakery. Although 3rd Street was a highly used road due to the number of parking garages and the streetcar, the entrances to the shops on this side all appeared to be back doors with signs differentiating one from the others. Considering the other side opened up into the Farmer's Market, it was understandable that this would be the back entrance for deliveries. In addition to the numbered signs by the green doors, the second story displayed banners with the names or other things they were known for. I couldn't help but wonder what lay on the other side of the door under the banner that read, "Best Flour in the City." Kendrick possessed a one-track mind when his stomach was empty, so I followed him through one of the two doors marked for the Bloom Baking Company.

The chalkboard menu added an element of homeyness to the small space. Kendrick eyed the line and told me, "Why don't I stay here and get the food while you find an empty table outside somewhere?" How uncharacteristic of him to let me go out on my own the day after an altercation such as yesterday's at the gym. Maybe he was making an effort to reduce his overprotectiveness.

I wandered out the front door toward Main Street, having remembered seeing additional tables on that side of the buildings when looking out the window of the streetcar. Once I'd claimed the table, I texted specific directions to Kendrick of my whereabouts. Now that it was over, it was hard to remember or imagine a time when these streets would have been empty during the beginning of the pandemic. Every once in a while, I found photos that were taken during that time featuring the deserted sidewalks.

"Marco!" Kendrick's voice echoed off the brick exteriors that differentiated the back of the stores from the storefront. At least he had headed in the right direction, even though he hadn't quite found me yet.

The few people who had heard him turned in his direction with amused expressions. "Polo!" I said in response, and the onlookers appeared even more intrigued. Whether we wanted to or not, we would likely have an audience while eating our goodies.

"As soon as you walked away, I forgot what you told me you wanted, so I made an educated guess based on past experiences," he said apologetically. "A cappuccino and an almond croissant since I know you love croissants."

"Now that I think about it, I'm not sure if I even told you what I wanted," I said, "but that sounds perfect to me. What did you get?" I eyed the other drink and the bag that he hadn't set down in front of me.

"I also got a cappuccino, so don't get any bright ideas about that," he said before opening the bag. "I got a spinach and feta pie because I knew you'd want to try some and a pineapple danish. Those pastries were all very tempting, but with ice cream on the list for later, I passed on the tarts. We're coming back here though until we try everything on that menu."

I glanced at the sign for the City Market Coffee House that we hadn't even made it into. "You know, if you wanted a healthier breakfast, we probably should have avoided the bakery and walked further to the coffee shop. I've heard they also make smoothies and breakfast burritos." The croissant was flaky and delicious and everything this Saturday morning needed. Combined with the coffee, today was shaping up to be much better than yesterday.

"If we were eating breakfast burritos, you wouldn't have that goofy smile on your face," Kendrick said and broke off a piece of the danish for me to try.

Until now, I'd successfully been keeping my thoughts from drifting back to our interrupted exchange last night. I couldn't think of any better way to bring it up again than to ask. "Last night you said that it would be hard for you if I dated Luca. Why is that?"

Kendrick paused mid-sip as if he'd been caught. "Well, our friendship dynamic has always been hard to navigate when one of us was dating someone else," he tried to explain, but the confusion must have been evident on my face. "Do you remember what it was like in high school when I dated? Some of those girls were horrible to you. Yeah, it helped me to see that I didn't want to waste my time with them, but usually, the person trying to have a relationship with one of us struggled with our friendship."

"What about Sarah?" I asked though I wasn't sure how the conversation was taking this turn. His response wasn't the admission I was wanting to hear.

"I never told you this, but she wasn't as comfortable with how close we were as I wanted you to think," he said in explanation. "Honestly, I assumed that she would either learn to live with it or she and I would break up. The distance thing just made it easier for me since she didn't seem to be changing her mind."

"I never noticed that she felt uncomfortable with me," I said while trying to remember a time that I might have misinterpreted her words or actions. Hindsight might be 20/20, but Sarah must have been talented in hiding her misgivings.

Kendrick pulled two plastic forks out for us to share the savory part of our breakfast. "It's not that she didn't like you," he explained, "but more that she didn't know how to handle my having a best friend who's a girl. For a while, I thought she was overreacting, but there may have been some truth behind her insecurities."

Truth? Did he know the way that my heart raced or jumped in my chest whenever I saw him? Or was he aware of the subconscious way my eyes followed him when we were in the same room together? Was the truth, the fact that his kiss had set fire to the kindling that I had been collecting for years, written all over my face like an open book that he had been reading over and over again since high school? There was no way to know the answers to the million questions that swarmed my mind unless I decided to be brave and leap.

"Kendrick, I think I'm in love with you," I blurted out and then corrected myself by adding, "In fact, I know that I'm in love with you." I had fantasized about this moment countless times, having pictured all the possible reactions he would have. I assumed that knowing someone for over ten years meant that he would have been predictable enough that I could prepare for any outcome, but even Kendrick had managed to surprise me from time to time.

He put down his fork and focused his full attention on me. "I'm kind of mad at myself now," he said, a line I would have never conjured up in my imagination. "I should have been the one to be straightforward with you and to tell you how I feel, and instead I've been letting my insecurities cloud my head with doubt. The truth behind Sarah and all the other failed relationships of mine is that there's a part of me that has always held onto the idea that you're the one I would end up with.

"But then Luca came along, and the idea of you with someone else freaked me out. I didn't want to get in the way of your being happy, so I backed off on any intentions I had other than remaining friends with you. That kiss made things much more complicated because now when I see you, all I want is to relive that moment. You're really in love with me?"

"I've been in love with you for as long as I can remember," I admitted, and I wasn't sure whether I would have held that back if I could. It felt as if a weight had been lifted in being able to share the one secret I'd been keeping from my best friend.

"I don't even know the moment I fell in love with you," he said sheepishly. "One day, I just knew it and couldn't shake it. I should have told you months ago, but I didn't want to risk losing you if you didn't feel the same way. It's hard to face reality when you've built up a fantasy in your head for years of how things could be. I felt pretty lost while you were in Ireland because you're such a big part of my life that I didn't know what to do without you."

"Without me, you would be wandering around the grocery store unsure of what you need because I wasn't there with a list," I said with a smile that I couldn't suppress. Kendrick was in love with me and wanted a future with me.

He stood up from his seat and reached out a hand to help me up. I glanced at my half-full cup of cappuccino and shot him a questioning expression. "I've been trying to be polite by waiting for you to finish your coffee first, but I'll just buy you another one if this gets too cold," he said and pulled me from my seat and into his arms. His lips crashed into mine as if he'd been waiting his whole life for this moment, which he unmistakably had. Still, this kiss was gentler than the first, one that exuded love and adoration. When he released my lips, he sprinkled other parts of my face with kisses before shifting us into a hug.

"I have to tell you something else, but it can wait until later," I whispered and pushed it from my mind so that I wouldn't tell him now.

"Just so we're clear, you're my girlfriend now, right?" he asked as he let me go and collected our trash. "Because I'd rather tell Mikey and Reagan before they catch us kissing or something."

His reminder of that moment brought up something else I'd been waiting to say to him. "Speaking of which, you lectured Mikey about how people who are just friends don't make out like that, yet you let all this time go by without bringing up our kiss to me," I pointed out to him before taking the last sip of my drink.

"As I said, I've been letting my insecurities cloud my judgment on things, including that," he replied. "I only talked about it with Mikey because I wanted to know if he'd ever had an experience when he kissed a girl and thought it was amazing, but it wasn't as good for her. It was my way of finding out whether chemistry like that could be one-sided, or if it had to be something you also felt. Truthfully, I was doing what I could to save myself possible embarrassment."

"You could have just told me," I insisted, but I could relate to his hesitancy. "It's so weird how having feelings for each other made us feel like we couldn't talk to each other about it even though we've been talking to each other about everything else for years."

"I wasn't exactly forthcoming about the stuff going on with my mom either, but it's tied into my inability to stop thinking about you. Okay, enough of this back and forth. We should start walking toward the museum since it opens in five minutes."

I hadn't been paying attention to the time. Our River Market agenda seemed inconsequential compared to how drastically my future had changed over breakfast. Our future. A future that would likely lead to a wedding and a house and children. Our children. Boys and girls with my dark curly hair and his blue eyes. It was all too real now, not a far-off "what-if" that my sixteen-year-old self would wonder about. How did one simply date a guy that she already knew like the back of her hand?

With our fingers linked, we walked east on 3rd Street toward Grand Boulevard and the museum's entrance. I could have been floating for all I knew. Every time I snuck a glance at Kendrick, it struck me all over again that he was mine. He might have been glowing from happiness, or it might have merely been the way the sunlight was hitting his face.

"You can stare at me all you want later," Kendrick said, "but right now we're going to stick to the plan. All your scenarios about our lives can wait until later." I tuned in to the present again, ready for the videos and movies that would explain the story behind the museum. After its sinking, Steamboat *Arabia* had been lost for over 130 years, preserving artifacts that were dated from before the Civil War. Over that period, erosion had moved the river's course enough that when they located the ship, it was no longer in the channel. I could tell that the idea of rivers changing course like that fascinated Kendrick's engineering mind.

The way that they could salvage the cargo from a sunken ship reminded me of the *Titanic* when they uncovered treasures that had been onboard. Of course, excavating a steamboat from 45 feet underground seemed to be an easier feat than raising the *Titanic* from the bottom of the ocean as some have desired to do. These artifacts dated back further than that of the *Titanic* and this ship was thought to have carried gold and fine china. Perhaps the reason Steamboat *Arabia* wasn't as well known as the *Titanic* was simply the differences. The *Titanic* had boasted the inability to sink, thus warnings weren't taken seriously, while steamboats were known to sometimes perish in the waters of the Missouri River due to random trees that had fallen and were out of sight. No one perished in the sinking of the steamboat the way many aboard the *Titanic* had. To me, the difference was in how seriously one thought the risk of danger was.

"You know, the fact that only an animal was a casualty in the *Arabia* sinking makes the *Titanic* incident, which took place over 50 years later, seem absurd," I expressed out loud to Kendrick. A few others in the museum had amused expressions on their faces from my comment as if they had been thinking the same.

"If you're going to compare the two, keep in mind that the steamboat was intended mostly for cargo unlike the *Titanic* which was built for luxury," he said, clearly entertained by the tangent my train of thought had been on while looking at the artifacts on display. "That doesn't justify the fact that a ship built for luxury should have been equipped with enough lifeboats for all on board. Full-speed ahead into a minefield of icebergs while knowingly not having enough safety plans in place would cause a huge lawsuit nowadays."

Though I was in a museum looking at artifacts from a steamboat, I found myself on my phone doing a brief search on any lawsuits involved with the *Titanic*. "The legal courts back then made it harder for victims to be compensated for the company's negligence," I summarized my findings. Having satisfied my curiosity, I slipped my phone into my back pocket and intertwined my fingers with his again.

"You owe me $20," I heard a familiar voice say from behind me. Kendrick must have picked up on it too because we both turned around at the same time, coming face-to-face with Mikey and Reagan. Mikey gave a wave and accelerated his pace to join us.

"I guess I'm paying for lunch today," Reagan complied, directing her response to Mikey.

Noticing that Kendrick and I were waiting for an explanation, Mikey said, "I bet Reagan that today would be the day that you two finally ended up together. Last I checked, people who are just friends don't hold hands like that." He gestured to our linked fingers with a smug expression directed at Reagan.

"Nice of you to join us," Kendrick said to them with a smile, but I could tell that the nicety was a bit forced.

It wasn't that I minded our friends hanging out with us, but it was also great having Kendrick all to myself. Then, I recalled what Reagan had told me about how double dating would keep her and Mikey from moving too quickly physically. Their showing up was likely a subtle ploy to use us to keep them accountable. Granted, there were cheaper ways to keep their hands off each other, ones that weren't $15 each for admission. Kendrick and I didn't have to communicate to know that any plans we had made beyond the museum were now subject to change.

Once our group concluded our museum visit, the guys and girls split up for a restroom break. Now that I was alone with Reagan, I couldn't hold back the slight annoyance at how the two invited themselves to join us.

"You couldn't let us have one day to ourselves?" I asked her.

"I thought you guys wanted us to join you," she said with evident confusion.

I replayed last night's elevator conversation in my head as best as my memory would allow. "If my memory is correct, Kendrick had asked me what time I wanted to leave, and you and Mikey were the ones debating on inviting yourselves," I said to her.

She paused for a moment, trying to think through the same exchange before she facepalmed herself. "You're right," she groaned. "I had assumed that if you two were discussing your plans in front of us, it meant that it was an open invite. I didn't even ask, and I should have. Is this what it's going to be like for us now that we're roommates dating two guys who are also roommates and cousins? Having to over-clarify which activities are group dates and which ones are intended as one-on-one dates."

"I think being in serious relationships will require all of us to sharpen our communication skills," I said to her. Given how long Kendrick and I danced around our feelings for each other, even he and I could learn how to better express our thoughts and intentions to each other.

"You know what I think?" she asked though it was a rhetorical question that she would answer without any guesses offered from me. "Ireland was good for you. Really good for you. Since we started college together, you've been more passive about what happens to you in life, as if things were happening to you and you were reacting to those situations. When it came to people that you love and care about, you would take action and intervene, as you had with me, but in things that involved you personally, you were very conflict-avoidant. Lately, something has changed about you, and I happen to be a fan of those changes, even when the things that need to be changed are directed at me." As far-fetched as the Blarney Stone theory was, if Mikey could believe it, so could she.

"My theory is that the powers I gained from kissing the Blarney Stone have rendered it nearly impossible to keep my mouth shut sometimes," I confessed to her, keeping my tone light in case she thought the idea was ridiculous.

"Hey, if a legend were to come true for anyone, it would be you," she responded with a shrug. "You needed all the help you could get."

CHAPTER FOURTEEN

"Mom?" Kendrick called out from the front door of his parents' house, his backpack slung over one shoulder. Earlier this week, he had let his parents know that we were coming to visit for the weekend. Both his mom's and dad's cars were parked in the open garage, and he had used his key to unlock the front door. His youngest sister Kennedy was the first to appear at the top of the stairs in the entryway.

"They're in the backyard pulling weeds," she informed us while bounding down the stairs to hug her big brother. "Ariella, are you staying with us too?" Her big blue eyes begged me to stay, identical to the ones Kendrick sometimes gave me when I insisted that I needed to go to bed early rather than watch another episode of one of our shared TV shows. Fortunately, I had years of training saying no to those eyes whenever necessary.

"Sorry, Kennedy, but I already promised my parents that I would stay with them while I'm in town," I said to her gently. She gave a pout, but still hugged me anyway.

After a door somewhere else in the house opened and closed again, we heard barking gradually get louder until Kendrick's dog ran toward him. By the time the golden lab could smell us and recognize us, her tail was wagging with excitement. Given that it had been years since my last visit to the Barlow house, his dog had gotten older. I had been hanging out with him here the day his parents brought her home as a puppy to surprise their son. Now, his sisters had taken over the responsibility for her even though our apartment complex was pet-friendly.

"Have you thought about taking her back to the city to live with you and Mikey?" I asked him as the dog followed us through the house.

"Every time I come home for the holidays or a weekend visit, I'm tempted to bring her back with me," he admitted as he stooped to pet the lab again, burying his face in her fur. "I don't think she would adjust well to being in an apartment by herself all day. She's used to being in a house full of people, only left alone for a few hours a couple of days a week. Not to mention that there's a backyard here where she can run around and get exercise. Living in an apartment with a dog is hard to do, especially if it's a larger breed that needs to be walked a certain distance every day. I believe it's healthier for them if they have more space." There he was tugging on my heartstrings with how selfless he could be, even when it came to his beloved dog.

With the ground soft and muddy from yesterday's rain, Kendrick's parents had taken full advantage of the ideal weed-pulling conditions. His mother likely spent the better part of her day in the garden, and her husband must have joined her when he arrived home after work. The summer sun was beginning to set on this Friday evening, the sky picturesque in its display of pinks and oranges. Making sure the dog didn't follow us outside through the mud, we slipped through the back glass door onto the wooden deck. The noise was loud enough to alert his parents to our presence.

"Carson, our baby boy is here!" Mrs. Barlow exclaimed to her husband as if he couldn't see Kendrick with his own eyes. Excitement often overshadowed logic in these situations though.

"And he brought our favorite free-loader with him," Mr. Barlow teased, winking at me. Kendrick's looks were the perfect combination of genetics passed down from his parents, his brilliant blue eyes a reflection of his mother's kind ones and his father's dark hair, now sprinkled with gray. I had always assumed that the way his hair curled when he was due for a haircut was a recessive gene, but his mother's strawberry blonde hair was naturally curly though she usually straightened it. Today, her curls were pulled back into a bun to keep her hair off her neck while gardening.

"Hi, Mom and Dad," Kendrick greeted his parents. He hugged each of them, not caring if they were covered in sweat and dirt. "What's for dinner?"

As if on cue, Kendrick's stomach growled. "Well, we were planning on going to that Mexican restaurant you like. Your mom and I just need to clean up, and then we'll be ready to go. Ariella, you're welcome to join us if you'd like."

"I'd love to," I said to them with a smile. "Kendrick, is it okay if we drop my stuff off at my parents' house before heading to the restaurant?"

"Why don't you take my car and meet us there?" he said as he pulled his keys from his pocket to give to me. "I can ride over with my family." While most girls would have misinterpreted his suggestion as a sign that he wanted a short break, my history with Kendrick gave me a better perspective. If there was one thing, apart from me and his family, that he was overprotective about, it was his car. His Volvo was possibly his most-prized possession and a gift from his father. This wasn't a move to temporarily get rid of me, but rather a gesture of trust. His parents seemed to interpret the interaction in the same way because Mrs. Barlow gave her husband an inquisitive expression.

I accepted his keys and set my course toward the Volvo. The drive from his childhood home to mine was only seven minutes. We had timed it so many times in high school, and no matter how busy the stop sign and one traffic light in between were, we always seemed to make it in seven minutes barring extenuating circumstances involving snow and ice. Neither of my parents nor my brother was home, but the calendar that hung in the kitchen was marked with a soccer game on today's date. I carried my weekender bag from the Volvo's trunk into my former bedroom. I was freshening up in the bathroom when Kendrick texted me.

KENDRICK

We're heading to the restaurant now. See you soon.

I pictured Kendrick crawling in the back seat of his mom's minivan the way he had as a teenager when they were going on family trips. Though he was the same height he had been as a high school senior, the added bulk from his gained muscle made the image in my head rather comical. When I pulled into the parking lot of Los Tacos Cantina Grill, I parked next to the Barlow minivan. Kendrick was waiting for me at the entrance to lead me to the table where his family had been seated. It was strange to look at the table that contained one less child than usual. The oldest of the three girls was away for her last year of college, I remembered, suddenly feeling old. At the time we both moved away for college, the youngest, Kennedy, was only five. Now she was thirteen, seemingly grown up overnight.

Kendrick, my boyfriend (because I got to call him that now), pulled out the chair from the table for me, exhibiting the manners his mother had taught him growing up. All of them watched us with smirks on their faces, but he didn't seem to notice the glimpses from his family.

After taking our drink orders, Kendrick said to everyone, "So, I have more than one reason for wanting to come visit this weekend. Of course, my main reason was to celebrate Mom's clean bill of health with all of you, but I also wanted to share something with you in person." I braced myself for the announcement that I knew would come. He and I had both agreed that we wanted to tell our families about our change in relationship in person rather than over the phone.

“If you’re going to tell us that you and Ariella are dating, we already knew,” Kennedy interjected in a sassy tone. Kendrick looked deflated at his youngest sister’s remark.

“Yeah, it’s not like it was a huge secret that you two liked each other,” Kristen, the second youngest, said. “It was only a matter of time.”

“I’m surprised it took this long,” Mr. Barlow said.

Kendrick’s eyes shifted from one family member to the next, taking in the lack of shock on all of their faces. He asked them, “How did you know for sure it had happened if you’ve been waiting for it all this time?”

“Kendrick, you let her drive your car,” his mom said, confirming my earlier thoughts. “You would never let a girl you’re not serious about drive your car. Even when you two were still just friends, you would have driven her yourself rather than suggest she take your keys. A mother knows her son.”

Kennedy looked like she was about to burst from whatever secret she was hiding. Kendrick stared her down in the way older siblings could to the younger ones to get them to crack. After nearly thirty seconds, she caved and confessed, “I was looking out my bedroom window when I heard your car pull up, and I saw you and Ariella kissing.”

Kendrick’s face flushed pink at the revelation of his younger sister witnessing our kiss. There was nothing immodest about it, but it wasn’t the example he would have wanted to set for his thirteen-year-old sister. With how long I had been practically family to her, I might as well have been married to her brother by this point.

Kristen spoke up before I could, "Kendrick, we're not little kids anymore who need constant protection and sheltering. Kennedy isn't going to go around school kissing all the boys just because she saw you, a responsible adult in your 20s, kiss your girlfriend whom all of us have known for years. If anything, it's kind of a relief to know that our big brother isn't going to end up alone. I'm looking forward to being in the wedding."

As far as timing was concerned, her last sentence could be considered either horrible timing or perfect timing. It was said right after Kendrick had taken a drink of his water, resulting in his spitting out that water due to his astonishment. Kristen wore the smugness of one proud of her accomplishment. Definitely on purpose.

"We haven't discussed that much yet," I said for Kendrick as he tried to regain his composure. "It's not that we haven't talked about it at all, but we're getting used to the change from friendship to dating, and a wedding still seems like more of an abstract idea for the future. I'm sure as time passes, it'll become more of a reality. We're not in any rush to get to the altar or any of the things that come with that." He squeezed my hand under the table in gratitude for helping explain.

Tonight, my words were enough to pacify the curiosity emanating from his family. Soon—sooner than either of us would likely be ready for—both our families could become impatient. While I would be subject to a fraction of the pressure, the majority of the questions regarding a proposal would all be directed at him. Kendrick had never been one to need my protection, and he could hold his own against the hints in the coming months.

I turned to smile at him, and my breath caught at how incredibly handsome he was when he looked at me adoringly. It was almost overwhelming enough to make me forget that we were surrounded by his family in a restaurant. If ten years hadn't lessened how much I wanted to marry him, another few months or even a year would only increase that desire. He could propose to me tonight, and I would say yes. We didn't need time because we were unsure about each other, but because it would take time and saving money to be financially set for that next step. Mikey and Reagan would both have to figure out new living arrangements as well.

"Have the lovebirds spilled the beans yet?" I heard an all-too-familiar voice ask from a few feet behind me. I turned around to find my own family as if they had prior knowledge of our whereabouts...because my family had been told we would be here, and based on my mother's question, my and Kendrick's parents had discussed our relationship before our arrival. He put the pieces together a few seconds after I had, the lightbulb moment evident across his face.

"I'm afraid that Kennedy beat them to the punch," Mr. Barlow said with a laugh. "Come join us, we have room for three more." My father, mother, and younger brother, with the assistance of the restaurant staff, pulled up chairs and gave their orders. The scene that played out before me was a little too scripted to be considered a spontaneous coincidence. This dinner was undoubtedly staged by our parents.

Sensing my unease, Kendrick whispered in my ear, "If both of our families already knew and are this cavalier about it, it's a good sign. It means that no one has any objections to the possibility of becoming one big family in the future." While having their approval would make life smoother, the biggest influence on our future together was whether he wanted it as much as I did.

Though my older sister and Kendrick's oldest sister were both absent from the large table, the Barlows and Stewarts who were present melded together as if being one wasn't just a future goal. Kendrick had been my best friend all these years, but I hadn't thought about how our friendship had also forged bonds between our parents and siblings. An official merging would be nearly effortless.

After dinner, our two families separated to their respective homes, leaving Kendrick and me alone in the parking lot with his Volvo. He had promised my father that he would drop me home in another hour before he whisked me away to the largest park in town for an evening stroll along the paved trail.

"I still have a hard time believing that the Blarney Stone is to blame for your confessing your feelings first," Kendrick said as we walked hand-in-hand through the summer air.

"I don't know what else to tell you," I said with a smile. "Mikey and Reagan have no problem believing that the Gift of Gab is behind my sudden outspokenness. Even Kathleen can see that there might be some validity to it."

"It's not that I don't believe in magic or supernatural entities affecting the physical," he explained, "but for most of the time that I've known you, you've never been that timid with me. Apart from the being in love with me thing, you've never kept secrets from me. I've seen you stand up for yourself and be bold when the situation calls for it. Granted, you're not nearly as outspoken as others, but you're certainly not shy in my eyes. I would argue that the real reason you beat me to it was more about my fear of losing you."

As much as I hated to bring it up, I needed a solid example to prove my point to him. "What about the time that I told you that I thought Luca was hot?" I pointed out, grateful that the dark would hide his reaction to my mentioning another guy. "Why would I admit that to you when I was still unsure about your feelings for me? It's one thing to say that when you're secure in your relationship with someone, but there's no way that I would have confessed that to you then."

"Okay, your logic checks out on that one," he admitted. "But how does that explain how long you went without bringing up our kiss?"

"I still have control over my thoughts even though I can't control what comes out of my mouth," I said. The concept of it still baffled me at times. Most people had control over both what they thought and what they said, whether they wanted to admit it or not. "If I want to have full control over what I say, I have to be on guard with my mind and what I allow myself to think about."

He stopped walking, pulling me close to him under the moonlight. "I guess that would be the flip side to speaking your mind. In all honesty, I don't care if it's magical powers or just that you're becoming more confident and bold. I love both sides of you and how the fact that you can still be both makes you unpredictable. Yet you're also predictable enough that I can count on you and trust you with my heart."

"Does it freak you out when our parents start talking about weddings and babies?" I asked him.

"Babies?" he said, the nervousness evident in his tone. "I don't recall anyone mentioning anything about babies."

"They didn't, but you and I both know that as soon as there's a ring and a wedding, that'll be all our parents will talk about," I nearly groaned as I buried my face in his chest. "How can everything be happening too fast and too slow at the same time?"

"That's the price to pay for falling in love with someone you've been best friends with for years," he said and wrapped his arms around me.

I pulled away just enough to look at his shadowed features in the moonlight. "You never answered the part about weddings."

He slowly kissed my forehead, taking his time to answer my pestering. "The idea of marrying you makes me happier than you could ever know. I wouldn't be doing all this if I didn't see myself spending the rest of my life with you. Weren't you the one who told my parents only an hour ago that there's no rush?"

"I just want to make sure we're on the same page," I said to him, content with this present moment.

His eyes almost glowed in what little light enveloped us. What I didn't know all those years I assumed it was unrequited love was that once we did find ourselves here, I would constantly find new things about Kendrick to love. If we were just friends, I wouldn't know I could love the way his eyes intensified before he leaned in to kiss me. When we were just friends, I didn't get to relish in the taste of his lips, drowning deeper and deeper. His kiss was like its own type of magic, rendering me useless and time endless. Somewhere in the abyss of my mind, another memory from Ireland resurfaced.

"What?" he asked when I broke out into a smile. But then his lips occupied mine with his own again as if he weren't anticipating a response. Or he wanted to kiss me more than he wanted to know what I was thinking right then.

I let him take the lead for a few more seconds before breaking the kiss again to answer. "I wished for you at the wishing steps."

"You wished for me at the wishing steps?" he repeated in question. "You mean you could have wished for anything, and you wished for something that was already yours?"

I glared at him and broke free of his grasp to continue walking the trail back to his car. He stood there for a few seconds and then jogged to catch up with me. Slightly out of breath from my sprint, I turned to him and said, "You were thousands of miles away chatting with other girls on a dating app, so yes, out of everything I could think to wish for, I wished for you."

He pulled me into his arms, his lips brushing my hair as he explained, "I was running away from my feelings for you while failing to stop myself from comparing all the girls out there to you. You set the bar pretty high, you know? I might have saved myself all the trouble if I had tried kissing you before signing up for that stupid dating app. I should have picked you up at the airport and kissed you then and there."

"It's not that hard to call you by your first name, Kendrick," I said teasingly.

He laughed, "It's so much more than that. Even the way you say my name sounds unique, like a siren's call."

I breathed in his scent and memorized his steady heartbeat as my head rested against his chest. I waited until we were inside his car to ask him the lingering question I still held back by dismissing it from the forefront of my thoughts. "Was that first kiss really just a way to hide in plain sight from Sullivan, or had you been waiting for an excuse to kiss me?"

The streetlights and moonlight illuminated his face enough for me to see his glowing smile in the near-darkness. "I wanted to kiss you so badly that when we were in that moment of panic, I didn't second guess the idea. So, a little of both. But more the second. If I had planned it better, I would have made sure it was more romantic."

"It was perfect," I assured him. And it was because it was part of our journey. It was perfect because it was Kendrick.

Kendrick shifted his Volvo into park in my parents' driveway but didn't rush out of the car. Even when we were platonic friends in high school, Kendrick would always get out of the car and walk me to my door when he was ready to say goodnight.

"I think I might be slightly afraid of your dad," he admitted before he sighed and rested his head against the headrest.

I laughed lightly at his statement before I said, "Why? My dad loves you. He was nice to Sullivan, and we all know he likely only tolerated Sullivan."

"Like father, like daughter," Kendrick said with a smile, and he was right in both instances.

"My father doesn't quite love you as much as I do, but you certainly don't have anything to be afraid of," I said to reassure him. "Just as long as we don't do anything crazy like go to Vegas and elope or take ten years to get married, you'll be his favorite child-adjacent."

Kendrick turned his car off as he said, "I am morally opposed to both of those scenarios. The only Elvis I'll allow at our wedding is 'Can't Help Falling In Love,' and I don't have the patience to wait ten years to make you my wife. Five years is too long. Three years is too long. I guess I should start sucking up to your dad now."

I shook my head as Kendrick opened the door and burst out his side of the car to rush around to open the front passenger door for me. "You're not going to kiss me goodnight?" I pouted as I walked up the front steps with him.

"Your dad installed a doorbell camera," Kendrick said as his head gestured to the gift my siblings and I had given my dad last Christmas. "He can easily spy on us. There's a reason I've always been one of his favorites." My boyfriend chastely kissed my cheek and waited for me to unlock the front door before he headed back to his car.

The small foyer by the front door was dark, but the lamp in the living room next to my dad's recliner was still on. My dad was naturally a night owl, though he sometimes dozed off in the recliner for a few minutes before finally going to bed for the night. I assumed he must have been napping, but then he said, "Kendrick's right. There's a reason he's one of my favorites. He's always been a good boy."

CHAPTER FIFTEEN

Kendrick took the initiative of reporting our relationship to HR at the office. When word reached Li Jun of our declared relationship, he simply looked at us and said, "I didn't realize that you two weren't already dating," before shrugging it off. Showing up to work together every day since we had both started working here must have given him that impression.

Hannah, having overheard the news, winked at me and gave me a thumbs-up. "Way to snatch him up," she said to me as her way of congratulations.

When Kendrick and I sat down at lunch, Luca gave an approving nod, "I much prefer being the third wheel at lunch than to have to try to keep quiet about your obvious feelings for each other."

Kendrick looked at me thoughtfully for a few seconds, contemplating something. Then he said to Luca, "Obviously, Ariella is off-limits now since she's my girlfriend, but she does have a sister who lives in Kansas City and is newly single again." I pictured Luca and my sister Kathleen together and wondered how I hadn't thought of that idea before Kendrick had brought it up.

I added, "Of course, no pressure or anything. We could just introduce you to her, and if nothing comes of it, no harm done. She's honestly the best older sister I could have asked for, and she's not had the best track record when it comes to boyfriends at no fault of her own except for her lack of discernment. Don't think of it as a set-up or blind date... more of a get-together to meet new friends."

"Game night," Kendrick suggested to both of us. I pulled out my phone to check Kathleen's synced calendar to ensure she wouldn't be traveling for work this coming Friday. Having confirmed she would be in town, I quickly typed out a text to her to see if she had plans.

Luca stared at us while we concocted our plan, finally relenting, "Fine, a game night sounds like a lot of fun, and with how often you two mention Mikey and Reagan, it would be nice to put faces to the names. I guess I should be flattered that you consider me a good candidate to introduce to your sister."

"She can't know that we did this on purpose though," I warned the two guys. "I already got more involved than I should have in the whole Sullivan debacle. This is just a casual game night."

After work during the streetcar ride to the apartment, Kendrick said, "You were the right level of involved in the Sullivan situation. Maybe the spying was a bit overboard, but from the beginning of the relationship, you were uneasy around him. I would have done the same—maybe even more—had that been one of my sisters. If Kathleen starts to suspect you're trying to set her up, I'll take the blame since I technically did state the idea out loud first. Trust me, your sister is less likely to be angry with me than with you." My phone lit up with a text notification from my sister.

KATHLEEN

A game night sounds perfect. I missed out on the big family dinner, so I still haven't gotten my turn to grill Kendrick about your relationship. Gotta make sure he's "future brother-in-law" material

Weren't you the one who purposely left me at school multiple times during my freshman year of high school so that Kendrick's mom would have to give me a ride home?

That doesn't sound like me. Besides, encouraging my sister to date her cute best friend in high school isn't nearly as serious as my fully adult sister dating the guy she's still best friends with after all those years of high school and college. This is the real deal now. My future nieces and nephews are at stake.

7 pm on Friday at Kendrick's apartment

"Kathleen has just confirmed her attendance on Friday night," I relayed to Kendrick. "She claims that she has yet to question your intentions toward me as if you weren't secretly her favorite between the two of us."

"If my plan works, she'll be too distracted by Luca to pay any attention to us," he said as he linked our hands together, fingers intertwined. The butterflies were still a fluttering mess in my stomach at the simplest touch. His small, kind gestures that had always been habit were magnified now that he was my boyfriend. I knew the intention and care behind them since I was privy to his feelings for me.

For the rest of the week, we planned the details of our get-together from the remainder of the guest list to the snacks and which games would be permitted on this particular night. Monopoly was quickly vetoed as well as Life since those both tended to last hours. Apples to Apples was a safe crowd-pleaser and icebreaker. Clue was one of my favorites among the classic games from our childhood. Settlers of Catan was a solid option but could be hard to play when the rules had to be explained to a newbie.

"Do I have to be the one to point out that Ariella kissed a rock before she kissed Kendrick?" Mikey said to us as we set out the snacks and board games at their kitchen island.

Rather than admonishing her boyfriend, Reagan added to his observation with a joke of her own, "Let's just hope that Kendrick kisses better than the Blarney Stone. Otherwise, it's only a matter of time before the Gift of Gab reveals the truth."

With my eyes on Kendrick, I stated truthfully, "I give him a 10 out of 10 most of the time."

"Most of the time?" he asked me incredulously.

Before my mind could think of anything to respond, Kathleen arrived, having invited herself inside. "I picked up the pizza on my way," she announced as she carried in the cardboard boxes containing the order I had placed an hour ago. Her statement was unnecessary given that the four of us who were already here were the ones hosting this shindig. I had been the one to ask her to pick up the pizza. Kendrick quickly stood up from his stool to relieve her of the pizza boxes. Once her arms were empty, she stepped over to the windows. "Wow, I forgot how nice your penthouse view of the city skyline is. I could get used to seeing this every morning and evening."

"It's one of my favorite things about this apartment," Kendrick agreed, his eyes locked with mine and a smile on his lips. "It's something I know I'll miss seeing when I'm married and living in the suburbs." Though we hadn't had a serious conversation about life beyond the apartment phase of our lives, the thought of having my own house—sharing a home with Kendrick—gave me a thrill of excitement about the future. The same must have crossed Kathleen's mind because she tore her attention from the view of the bustling city around us to me and Kendrick.

"You're not allowed to break up with my sister," she threatened with all seriousness. "If the two of you decide that it's better not to continue your relationship, then that's different since that would be a mutual decision that you came to together. But the two of you are too important to each other to break each other's hearts and leave. If one of you breaks the other's heart, you do what you can to fix it. Got it?"

Kendrick returned her stipulations, "I can't imagine my life without Ariella in it. I wouldn't do anything that could jeopardize this. I'm all in, no changing my mind. She's stuck with me for the rest of her life. I'm ready for this; we're ready for this."

Hearing those words made my heart feel so full I thought it might explode. It was the best type of overwhelming, like I was on the drop of a roller coaster with my adrenaline peaked and my body coursing through the air at unimaginable speeds. Kathleen seemed satisfied with his response, but Mikey couldn't help but ask, "Do I need to plan a trip to Vegas and start looking for a new apartment?"

"No!" Kendrick and I exclaimed at the same time.

"I want to be able to enjoy all stages of this," Kendrick continued. "I don't need to rush into marriage when I know I'm spending my whole life with her. Our families would kill us if we didn't have an engagement and a big wedding and all the things that come with that. Plus, I need time to save up for the ring Ariella wants but doesn't think I know about." I knew exactly which ring he was referring to, but I didn't know how he could have possibly found out about it.

"Vegas is overrated anyway," Luca's voice echoed from the front door of the apartment. A few seconds later, he appeared carrying a pan of dessert. "Tiramisu from my favorite Italian restaurant. Well, the favorite of the ones in Kansas City that I've tested so far."

I both wondered and asked, "Have you been ordering tiramisu from every Italian place you've visited?"

"That's genius," Mikey admitted thoughtfully. "You could create a scorecard of different factors that contribute to the perfect tiramisu and rate each one based on those traits. And then when you've determined the best tiramisu, you can do cannolis or gelato next."

Somewhere during Mikey's brainstorming, I witnessed the moment Luca and my sister locked eyes. The moment was subtle, but not entirely imperceptible to me. Kendrick had stealthily moved behind me to wrap his arms around me, his head resting on top of my own as we watched our friends and family around us. He whispered in my ear, "You saw that, right?" I nodded my head, a motion he would have felt against his chest with how closely he was holding me.

"Hi, I'm Luca," he introduced himself with his eyes still on Kathleen's even though this was also his first introduction to Mikey and Reagan. "I started working with Kendrick and Ariella a few weeks ago after moving here from Chicago." Luca finally shifted his gaze to Mikey and Reagan to nod at them in greeting.

I took the initiative to introduce the others to my fairly new co-worker. "That's Kendrick's cousin Mikey, his girlfriend Reagan who is also my roommate, and my older sister Kathleen."

"Are we waiting on anyone else?" Mikey asked me and Kendrick since we were the ones who had contacted possible guests for this game night.

Kendrick checked his phone. "Denver and Georgia can't make it because their babysitter canceled at the last minute."

"Wait," Luca said with an intrigued expression on his face, "His name is Denver like the city and her name is Georgia like the state? Are they married to each other?"

"Yes," Kendrick and I responded in unison.

Kathleen said, "Their names are actually how they ended up together. Someone thought it would be funny if they started dating, so they were set up on a blind date. Denver and Georgia also thought it was funny though, and they hit it off. Before you ask, their son's name is Austin like the city."

"I guess when you have a theme to follow, it can make choosing baby names easier," Luca said.

I looked up at Kendrick, the oldest of the children in his family. "It's names that start with K for my parents," he pointed out. "And to answer Mikey's question earlier, this should be everyone."

The next ten minutes were a flurry of activity as we all grabbed plates, slices of pizza, chips, and drinks before finding our places around the dining room table. Rather than take a vote to choose among our game options, Kendrick had written the name of each on a piece of paper and folded them up. He let Luca do the honor of randomly selecting one from a cup. In Kendrick's neat scrawl, I glimpsed the word "Catan" and knew we were in for an eventful night.

"Does everyone know how to play?" I asked the others as I walked over to the pile of games. The question was more for Luca since I'd played this with Kathleen, Mikey, and Reagan at past game nights.

"It's one of my favorites," Luca said in confirmation. We all took our places at the table; Kendrick and Luca were on either side of me.

KATHLEEN

Given your recent meddling in my personal life, I have to ask…did you invite me here to try to set me up with Luca?

It was Kendrick's idea, and I went along with it. If you're not interested, it's no big deal. He's new to Kansas City, so we thought it would also be a great way to introduce him to some of our friends

You do have eyes, right? I'd have to be stupid not to give a man who looks like that at least one date. I don't care whose idea it was. I appreciate that you thought of me and want to see me happy. It's flattering that you think I'd be a good match for him. Sullivan who?

You deserve the best. You're the one who dragged our family to Ireland and Blarney Castle. As annoying as the Gift of Gab might be, the least I can do is use it to make our lives better.

Under the table, Kendrick squeezed my hand. I couldn't have wished for a better life or better friends than the ones who sat around me. I pretended not to eavesdrop when Luca and my sister exchanged phone numbers so he could contact her with details about taking her out for dinner tomorrow night. She glowed with the promise of potential new love as I walked her to the elevator a few hours later. Mikey followed Reagan to the front door of our apartment, walking her home despite our living in the same building. Like I had all the other game nights before, I helped Kendrick clean up his kitchen and living room while watching him out of the corner of my eye. Unlike the previous times, he slowed me down with kisses. While I had always dreamed of our future together, the present moment was more than satisfactory.

CHAPTER SIXTEEN

The waitress set down two plates of tiramisu cheesecake at our table. As my fork glided through the layers of dessert, I couldn't help but feel proud of myself for a month of consistent workouts. Now that my promised month was up, I had no intention of stopping. Going to the gym with Kendrick gave me one more excuse to be around him, not that I needed any. We saw each other every day just like we had before we were dating, but now we had to make a conscious effort to do things separately. Kendrick would make plans with Mikey and Lucas on the same nights that I would hang out with Reagan and Kathleen.

"Worth the wait?" Kendrick asked me as he eyed the blissful satisfaction on my face.

"This cheesecake or you?" I asked because the serotonin coursing through my veins from the dessert was like what I felt when he kissed me.

Kendrick flashed me the smile that instantly melted me every time. "I know that I was worth the wait. Although, I sometimes wish we could have made this step sooner, mostly because I like kissing you a lot. Which makes me think I'll thoroughly enjoy being married to you and all the perks that'll come with that."

My mind flashed back to a memory from high school youth group during our freshman year when Kendrick and I both individually decided that we would both wait until marriage for sex. That commonality solidified our friendship throughout the years. When peers questioned our commitment to celibacy, we had each other and understood each other. It made navigating the dating world both easier and harder—easier because it weeded out the ones who weren't looking for anything serious but harder because it narrowed down the options significantly. Harder because it made me seem more intimidating as if I had impossible standards. Easier because it made it that much clearer that we were the best fit for each other.

"Is late next year too soon to get married?" I blurted. The question had barely registered in my thoughts before escaping my mouth.

"I was going to suggest we start looking at houses in the spring," he said with a shrug as if we were talking about the weather. "Our leases are up in September. Even if we didn't get married until later in the fall, one of us could move into the house before the wedding. The whole Mikey and Reagan aspect complicates it slightly."

I glanced at my left hand and imagined the engagement ring that I had not-so-secretly admired sitting on my ring finger.

"What are the chances that they would elope?" Although Reagan had become more responsible as of late, she was still naturally inclined toward spontaneity. Mikey was just the type who might indulge her in the last-minute Vegas trip he joked about regarding me and Kendrick.

Kendrick thought about my question as thoroughly as he would if I had asked him about one of his more challenging projects at work. "Surprisingly high, if I were to guess." With that realization, I mentally decided that Mikey and Reagan could figure things out for themselves regarding their living situations once Kendrick and I got married. As their friend, I wanted the absolute best for them, but I couldn't be the one making decisions or figuring things out for them.

"A little over a year from now isn't too soon?" I asked to be certain I wasn't the one controlling the timeline.

"Ariella," Kendrick said with that smile again, "I would marry you tonight if it wouldn't cause complete chaos for our close friends and family. You deserve to have the wedding and the ring you've dreamed about."

"As tempting as being married to you is, I'm content being your girlfriend right now," I assured him. "I'm still acclimating to the reality that I get to hold your hand and kiss you." On our way back to our apartments, he did those two things.

I don't think I can leave my apartment today. I'm struggling just to stand up straight right now.

I HADN'T BEEN the one to suggest or initiate it, but Kendrick kept track of when I was on my period. The habit had started in high school, particularly when I'd had excruciating cramps that sent me home from school early. Normally, I could still mostly function during that time of month, but occasionally, my uterus would wage a war I was ill-equipped to fight. After school that day, Kendrick showed up at my house with my favorite candy bar and notes from the classes I had missed.

Kendrick let himself into my apartment with his key rather than texting or knocking for me to unlock the door like he usually did. His key to my apartment was something he reserved for emergencies only. I remained in my spot on the couch as I waited for him to walk into the living room and witness my body in the fetal position wrapped in a blanket. Kendrick strode in with a large bag in one of his hands, and I instantly knew he had brought the usual supplies of dark chocolate and a heating pad.

"You really have loved me for a while," I said with a dreamy tone to my voice.

He froze at my words, a quizzical expression on his face. "Why do you say that?"

"Because you always come over to take care of me whenever I'm feeling terrible," I said with a small smile. "Not just when my cramps are unbearable, but you also came over the few times I've been sick and contagious. I gave you the flu last year."

He handed me the dark chocolate and set the heating pad on the coffee table before shoving his way into the little space I had left for him on the couch. I repositioned my head to rest in his lap. He played with my hair as he said, "I always felt like it was my job to take care of you. I would rather be sick with you than keep my distance for days anyway. Because I love you, and you're my favorite person to be around."

"You're better than chocolate," I said as I turned onto my back to look up at him. His blue eyes overrode my every thought. "I could look at you all day, every day, for the rest of my life, and I would still think you're the best-looking man I've ever seen. I just want to sit here and stare at you as I try to memorize your face so I can picture it perfectly when you're not around."

His hand caressed my cheek in peaceful silence as we continued to admire each other. "You have the perfect lips. It took a lot of self-control over the years to keep myself from kissing you. I think the only thing that held me back was the idea that I would get to kiss you eventually."

I shook my head with an amused expression plastered on my face. "We're so silly. Why did we dance around this for all those years? Either one of us should have made a move or something. All of high school and all of college and even a few years into full adulthood. We're just as bad as all the clichés in books and movies."

"Fear of rejection," Kendrick said as if it were inconsequential to the outcome. "I know you still don't believe me about this, but a lot of the guys in high school were too intimidated to ask you out. You were different from most of the other girls in a way that's attractive and somewhat scary. You're a forever-love kind of girl, not a mere first love. In hindsight, I wasn't mature enough to try to make you both. I thought that maybe if I kept myself in the friend zone, I could keep myself from falling for you. When I picked you up for senior prom—the moment I saw you—I knew that I would marry you one day."

I sat up so I could better address his confession. Eye to eye, his hand in mine, I told him the truth that was on my mind. "I know that stuffed dog was from you."

Kendrick smiled knowing exactly which one I had meant. He leaned in to brush his lips with mine, the kiss like a whisper before it turned tender and affectionate. The cramps that had been limiting me an hour ago were replaced with the butterflies that appeared every time he kissed me. His taste was addictive, and when he tried to pull away, I leaned in to capture his mouth again. Rather than resist me, his hand gently grabbed the spot where my jaw met my neck and urged me closer. Maybe we were so consumed by the kiss that we couldn't hear or maybe Reagan and Mikey had been trying to be quiet, but before either of us could break the spell, we heard our roommates clearing their throats.

"We got some Halo Top ice cream for all of us," Reagan said as she unpacked four pints from the grocery bag she had carried in. "Although, you're looking a lot more human than you did an hour ago." I would be embarrassed by the knowing smirk on her face, but it was hard to be embarrassed about kissing Kendrick. As far as I knew, I was one of the luckiest girls in the world because I got to kiss him. One glance at Kendrick's face, and it was clear he had no regrets about being caught. It was just Reagan and Mikey, after all.

"I'm just here for moral support," Mikey said, "I can't imagine what it must be like to go through that every month. It's no wonder Kendrick installed an app on his phone to keep track."

I turned to my boyfriend with a look of surprise. "You have a period tracker app on your phone?" I asked him. I had known he loosely kept track, but I wouldn't have guessed he had gone to that extent.

"Menstrual cycles can be an indication of possible health problems," Kendrick said in defense. "No offense, but you're horrible about going to the doctor for regular checkups. I just thought it couldn't hurt in case something unusual happens and you brush it off instead of talking to a doctor. It's also good information to have once we're married. Just knowing when you might be experiencing PMS symptoms has come in handy on many occasions."

"So if you notice that Kendrick is avoiding you around the same time every month, now you know why," Mikey said, his joke receiving glares from all three of us. "Just kidding. If anything, he's more whipped than usual."

Reagan came to Kendrick's rescue by telling her boyfriend, "Kendrick isn't whipped. When he's married, that's exactly the kind of behavior that'll earn him sexual favors."

Kendrick and I both flushed at Reagan's comment. "I don't expect anything in return when I do things for you, both now and when we're married," Kendrick said to me, though purposely louder than necessary for Reagan and Mikey to hear. "It's always ever been because I love you."

THE DECIBEL LEVEL around us triggered noise notifications from my smart watch as the air was electric with excitement. Arrowhead Stadium had a reputation that never failed to disappoint when the Chiefs were playing at home. Tonight was a long-anticipated game against a division rival and the first home game of the season. The September air was still warm with the residue of summer humidity, but the breeze brought some relief as the sun set in the distance.

Kendrick, Mikey, and Luca had started their own group message regarding football and home games on this season's schedule. Kendrick had been the first to suggest that they run any plans by "the women" in case we had an interest in going with them. Of course, all of us wanted to join them for this one. None of them seemed disappointed that their girlfriends were coming to a professional football game with them though. Kendrick even bought me a Mahomes jersey as if he had forgotten that when I had asked for one for Christmas, he had refused. Maybe getting Chiefs gear was one of the perks of my upgrade to girlfriend status.

"That was obvious defensive holding!" I yelled as if the referees could hear me and see the error of their lack of a penalty flag. Holding calls were rarely penalized consistently in the same game let alone from one game to the next.

"Babe, it's okay," Kendrick said to calm me down. "You can't expect them to catch every penalty in a game. They're just humans."

"I can see the holding from here," I argued in a quieter voice knowing he was right. The smirk on his handsome face revealed that he found my remark amusing. For years, he had tried to teach me all the ins and outs of the NFL from the basic rules to the penalties and positions. Now, he was seeing the fruit of his efforts in the form of my outrage.

The roar of boos from the spectators around us confirmed that I hadn't been the only one to notice. Kendrick squeezed my hand with a smile and a shake of his head. "Maybe the Blarney Stone did give you the Gift of Gab because the Ariella I've known for years would have kept her mouth shut."

I playfully punched his arm. While the teams on the field took a timeout, I glanced at our friends in the same row on the other side of Kendrick. Mikey was pointing out something to Reagan, possibly explaining something about the game to her. Luca and my sister weren't talking with their mouths, but the way they looked at each other every few seconds communicated more than words could. Over the years, I had witnessed every single one of my sister's relationships, and I had never seen her this happy or confident. Luca looked at my sister with the complete adoration that she deserved.

Despite the missed penalties, the Chiefs still came out as the winners with a 10-point margin. Our guys were on top of the world as the adrenaline seemed to spread throughout the crowds of fans like a transmissible disease. To the extroverts Mikey and Kendrick, it was more potent and energizing than injecting a double shot of espresso. Fortunately, the traffic leaving the Truman Sports Complex was enough to mellow out my boyfriend. By the time we reached the apartments, he was ready to crash.

"Thank you for coming with me tonight," he said with his sleepy smile. "It meant a lot to have you with me."

"Thank you for wanting me to come along," I said before I kissed him quickly on the lips in goodbye.

Mikey's energy level hadn't crashed quite as low as his cousin's had, and he guided Kendrick away from my front door and to the elevator. Before the doors could close, Kendrick yelled out, "I love you, Ariella!"

Embarrassed, I hurriedly closed my door and silently prayed that his display hadn't woken up any of our neighbors. Once safely in my room, I let the grin overtake my face. The smile remained plastered in place as I got ready to go to bed after what could only be described as the perfect day.

EPILOGUE

If you were to ask me, any city without mosquitos must be a paradise. That was exactly what I said when our guide pointed out the stone pines common in the Roman landscape. The umbrella-shaped trees were thought to be the reason that Rome was supposedly spared from the pests that cities like Venice had to combat. The internet seemed to be divided on whether the mosquitos were bad in Rome though, and stone pines were not on the list of plants known to repel mosquitos. I would have thought that a place without all the extreme cold of winter to kill the bugs would be constantly rampant with those pesky bloodsuckers. I couldn't help but wonder if stone pines would fare well if they were planted in Midwestern cities. Perhaps this particular type of pine didn't mix well with snow and ice.

"It's illegal to take plants or seeds from other countries back to the U.S.," Kendrick whispered in my ear as if he knew exactly what was going through my mind. Being in Italy was its own kind of dream, but exploring this country with my best friends—with my boyfriend—was another kind of otherworldly. It was every bit of fun as I imagined it would be. The sun here had already tanned his skin in a way that was hard to achieve spending forty hours a week working indoors. The golden glow of the sunlight lightened his dark brown hair and illuminated the blue of his irises. Gazing at him with the Italian architecture in the background made for a breathtaking image.

When I first brought up the possibility of Italy with Kendrick a few months ago, he was hesitant about traveling to a country known for its food. His problem wasn't that he disliked Italian food, but rather the opposite. He loved Italian cuisine almost as much as he loved keeping himself in physical shape. Upon our first walking tour though, he admitted that he would likely be burning as many calories with all the walking as he would be consuming at our meals.

Approaching the Spanish Steps from the top might have been lackluster from Kendrick's perspective, but from my previous research from various movies and virtual tours, I knew what to expect when the full Piazza di Spagna came into view. Unlike in the movies though, people were everywhere, making it impossible to take photos without capturing an innocent bystander in the digital memory. Fortunately, the rule forbidding sitting on the steps had been well enforced, limiting the crowd to standing only.

"Isn't it as amazing as I told you it would be?" I said to Kendrick with a blissful sigh. "I love everything about this country so far!"

"My favorite part is seeing how happy you are to be here," he replied as he linked his fingers with mine. "But yes, this lives up to the hype. I could pass on how crazy the drivers are here with their double parking and vespas, but some American cities could learn something from the public transportation systems here in Europe."

"Places like New York and Chicago have decent public transportation," I pointed out as I pulled my phone out of my pocket to take a photo of the Fontana della Barcaccia. "We just happen to live in a city that's spread out. They've been making improvements to the bus system as well as multiple extensions to the streetcar."

Our discussion was interrupted by the sound of our tour guide trying to capture the attention of the group, her yellow scarf catching the breeze on the small metal pole it was tied to. Around us, the multiple tour guides all carried similar scarves and flags in different colors as if they each had a claim on their color or pattern. The next stop was only a short walk away, and our guide used the opportunity to fill us in on the myths surrounding throwing coins into the Trevi Fountain.

As the legend went, tossing one coin meant that you would return to Rome, known as the Eternal City. Two coins were supposed to mean that you would fall in love, specifically with an attractive Italian. Three coins took it a step further with an additional promise that you would marry said Italian. While it might have seemed ridiculous to some, it was about as logical as tossing a coin into a fountain and making a wish. Given my history with old legends, I had already decided to test this one out while I was here.

Kendrick kept in step with me, pulling two coins from his wallet as we approached one of the most famous fountains in the world. "The way I see it," he began to explain, "I've already found the love of my life. Assuming we're on the same page, neither of us has any reason to throw more than one coin."

"Wait," I paused to meet his gaze. I could never tire of hearing him tell me. "Did you just say that I'm the love of your life?"

"Ariella Stewart, I love you, and I've been in love with you for as long as I remember," he declared somewhat sheepishly. "And in case I haven't made it clear, I have every intention of marrying you before the end of the year."

"I love you too," I said before kissing his cheek and wrapping my arms around him. "You're right, we already have each other. Hopefully, if we each throw in a coin at the same time, it means we'll get to come back together. I wouldn't be opposed to an Italian honeymoon."

Kendrick laughed as he released me from his embrace. "I'm not sure if I'll have much choice in the matter. If I remember correctly, you seem to be susceptible to these ancient legends. Not that I can complain since your last adventure played a role in how we ended up here together."

The Trevi Fountain, much like the Spanish Steps, was a common tourist attraction. It took a few minutes to maneuver our way through the crowds of people from various other countries, many speaking languages that my brain couldn't translate. Metal rails were constructed to focus the walking traffic toward the steps, but ducking under them and climbing the short drop proved to be a more efficient way to the fountain's edge.

"On three?" he asked as he dropped one coin in my hand. I nodded and we both turned our backs to the statues. With our right hands over our left shoulders, we simultaneously tossed our coins before taking photos to commemorate the moment. While this would have been fun to do with Reagan and Mikey, who were tired from the early morning activities at the Colosseum, part of me was glad that Kendrick and I were alone to share this magical moment. When we did find ourselves in Rome again (I knew better than to question the coin adage), only he and I would know our return was more than just another coincidence; it was a powerful combination of faith and courage.

As it turned out, there was a reason Mikey and Reagan hadn't been with us. Kendrick had arranged for a private table for us during dinner, separate from the remainder of our tour group. On the table next to my wineglass was a velvet box. Before the waiters had even reached our table to pour the wine, he was on one knee, holding out the box which displayed the diamond ring, a ring I had admired and failed to keep secret. When I said yes, our friends appeared with the musicians singing "Volare." Proposing to me in Rome was one way of guaranteeing that I would want to return, and I had a coin in the Trevi Fountain as a backup plan.

SIX MONTHS LATER, I witnessed Kendrick crying. In all the years I had known him, he had rarely cried. For some reason though, his reaction as he watched me walk down the aisle toward him was to shed a few tears. I could tell by my father's expression that Kendrick had just gained even more respect in his eyes. As the officiant addressed our guests, I gently wiped away those tears.

Although my makeup was supposed to be waterproof, Kathleen would kill me if I messed up her hard work. I was her masterpiece first and Kendrick's bride second. Once the vows and rings were exchanged, all bets were off though because Kendrick had no qualms about messing up my lipstick with our first kiss as husband and wife.

"You're my husband," I said in complete bliss.

"And you're my wife, as I always pictured you would be," he said before kissing me again. I had half a mind to skip the whole reception and spend the next few hours with my lips on his, but neither of our families would allow that. One of our siblings would find us no matter how well we hid. We still had some pictures to take and a cake to cut. Mrs. Barlow —my mother-in-law—had been looking forward to a dance with her only son since our engagement became official. This Mrs. Barlow—myself—wanted a first dance with the groom. Kissing would have to wait.

Kendrick watched me as my brain rested on the conclusion to follow through with the reception and everything that came with it. "Babe, we're going to be doing a lot of kissing for photos and toasts for the next few hours. The alone time we'll eventually get later is for the more-than-kissing."

He was correct. The thing I hadn't realized until I was the bride was that once the ceremony was over, I had no reason (apart from bathroom breaks and his dance with his mother) to leave Kendrick's side. We were expected to be glued to each other, constantly touching and kissing. Kendrick opted to do the garter toss simply because he knew how uncomfortable it would make me when he used his mouth to remove the thin piece of fabric from my thigh in front of our family. It didn't matter that our parents were already plotting the holiday schedule with their prospective grandchildren.

When I threw the bouquet, Kathleen and Reagan both caught it together. My sister let Reagan keep it knowing full well that Mikey had every intention of locking that down. They'd made it clear that neither of them wants the stress of a wedding, especially not one as close in time to ours.

During a short-lived moment of privacy, Kendrick whispered in my ear, "I can't wait to see you naked later." I gently hit him while shooting him the most unamused expression I could muster. "Hey, we're married people now. I'm supposed to want to see you, my wife, naked. Especially since I've been working out with you for the past year. I know you weren't that strict about your eating just for that dress. You would have looked incredible without all the extra effort."

"Maybe I wanted to watch my eating because I knew that I would be eating a lot during the honeymoon in Italy," I said arguing.

Months of dating followed by an engagement honed our non-verbal communication. Somehow, Kendrick had even discovered a facial expression that activated the Gift of Gab and reduced my filter to shambles. In our small, temporary bubble of privacy, he gave me the aforementioned expression.

I relented and said, "Fine, it was also partially because I wanted to look my best when you see me naked. I've seen you without a shirt on at the pool, and you're unfairly chiseled and attractive. It does help knowing that I'll be your first and only though. Unless I die before you, and then you have my permission to move on and be happy."

"Maybe we can die together like in that cheesy movie that always makes you cry," he said referring to The Notebook. Some of the greatest love stories spanned years before the protagonists stayed together.

I gazed longingly at the man I wanted to grow old with, the one I had essentially grown up with. Our bubble was burst by the sound of utensils clinking against glasses as guests signaled their desire for a kiss between the bride and groom. Kendrick proceeded to take my breath away with a dip kiss as he braced my body in his arms to keep me stable. Once he had me standing upright again, he winked at me, fully aware of his effect on me.

The speeches from the wedding party and our fathers had a common theme of "it's about time these two got married" and "it was obvious to everyone but them." Mikey recounted the moment he and Reagan witnessed the shift from friendship to more. Reagan joked about how Kendrick and I had always argued like an old married couple. My father shared about the evening when Kendrick had picked me up for the prom and the warning he had given my best friend, unbeknownst to me until this speech.

"I'm starting to think my father's threats might be the reason you waited so long to make a move," I whispered in my husband's ear as his fingers traced circles in my palm.

"He made it sound worse than it was," Kendrick said in my father's defense. "He told me to wait until I was certain I was ready for marriage. He suspected that we were each other's end game, but he wanted us to avoid the on-again-off-again mess that comes with being immature. It was sound advice, and I knew that I should listen to him if I wanted his blessing in the future."

We turned our attention back to my dad who was wrapping up his story. "When this boy—you'll always be that boy to me—came and told me that he wanted to propose to her in Italy, my only advice was that he shouldn't let the big, romantic gestures be a replacement for the small, everyday things he already does for her. My baby girl fell in love with the seemingly unnoticeable actions, not the big gestures. I'm delighted to call him part of the family because he's always made sure she's safe."

My sister was the last on the list to be handed the microphone, the grand finale for the wedding party speeches. Kathleen shot both of us a devious smirk before addressing our guests.

"Neither the bride nor groom knows this, but I was standing in the hallway on the first day they met in high school," Kathleen said. I could feel Kendrick's shock mirroring mine as his dancing fingers froze against my wrist. "They were assigned adjacent lockers during freshmen year, and I had the intention of checking in on my little sister. When I saw Kendrick at the locker next to hers, likely discussing whether they shared any classes, I had one thought: 'That boy is either going to break my sister's heart, or he's going to end up my brother-in-law one day.'

"It wasn't long after that he became a permanent fixture in her life, and I waited to see how long it would take for one of them to crack. I tried what I could to encourage Ariella or to hint to Kendrick that something more than platonic friendship was there, but nothing came of my efforts. Last year while on a family vacation in Ireland, I teased her about the obvious feelings she had been harboring for him as we made our wishes at the Wishing Steps. I was the one who pushed her to kiss the Blarney Stone, sending a ripple effect that would help these two finally—FINALLY—stop ignoring the fact that they were in love with each other.

"The real catalyst, though, was when they took it upon themselves to spy on my ex-boyfriend because they suspected he was cheating on me. My sister and her now-husband who protected me like a brother spent their Friday night in wigs. When they were almost caught, Kendrick kissed Ariella to hide their faces, but that kiss exposed all the feelings and pent-up attraction they had for each other. All of that to say, thank you for caring about me enough to put yourselves in an uncomfortable situation, but also, you're welcome for all the pushing. Ariella, I'm proud of you for finally going after what you want. If you decide to keep the 'K name' tradition for your kids, don't forget that my name starts with a K." Kathleen ended her speech with a wink in our direction and held her glass up to toast us.

Kendrick leaned into my ear and said, "I've been thinking that our kids should all have first names that start with A and middle names that start with K." *Our kids.* The idea of it still seemed far-fetched, but it was a likely reality in our near future.

For the remainder of the evening, I anchored myself in the present, enjoying every moment. Dancing and laughing and kissing and cake filled the seconds until it was time to make our departure. After hours of never being left alone, the low hum of the car engine was a welcome calm. Internally, I was at war between feeling excited enough to stay up all night and feeling tired enough to sleep for days.

As if reading my mind, Kendrick asked, "Want to get some drive-thru coffee on our way to the hotel? We should have opted for the coffee bar at the wedding reception."

"We wouldn't have had a chance to stand in line for coffee at our reception," I reminded him. "And yes, please. Can you see if they have espresso as an IV drip?"

His smile broke through my filters and defenses as it had countless times before. "Too much caffeine combined with nerves sounds like a bad idea. I'm only giving you enough to make sure you're awake for another two hours, not enough to keep you awake all week."

"I just want tonight to be perfect," I said as I avoided his gaze on my face. None of my facial expressions could hide my embarrassment from him. The drive-thru line ahead of us was a few cars long, but moving steadily.

"It's going to be weird and awkward. I have no such high expectations due to our inexperience. And I fully expect you to give me honest feedback on everything for the rest of our lives, including when I'm not putting my dirty socks in the hamper. But I also crave the moments when you're candid about how much you love me. If it took you kissing a stone for me to get to kiss you every day, I'll take all the other advantages and drawbacks that come with the Gift of Gab."

FLY ON THE WALL

KENDRICK

This idea of hers was absolutely insane, and yet I didn't have it in me to stop her. Harboring feelings for my best friend had always been a complicated balance, but lately, it had gotten more difficult to keep myself from spilling everything to her. Every time she sent me a photo from Ireland, I rushed to my phone like a desperate idiot. She's my ultimate weakness.

In all the years that I'd known Ariella, I hadn't figured out how to make a move. Instead, I took her shopping for somewhat realistic wigs as we discussed the details of our mission to spy on Sullivan. And yes, she looked hot in a blonde wig, but I still preferred her natural hair. She didn't need to change anything about herself to be more attractive. I could recognize her in any disguise, but I had years of practice and secret pining.

Before I could pull out my wallet, she paid for our wigs since this whole thing was her idea. In the end, it wouldn't matter because I would find a way to pay her back or treat her to something. We were never ones to keep track of "who owed whom."

Friday at work was a half day due to the original president's birthday. Funnily enough, his birthday became a bigger deal after he retired compared to when he was still working. Back then, it would have been a fifteen-minute break for cake before returning to whatever project deadline held priority that week. Now, the company catered lunch and gave everyone the afternoon off to take advantage of the early summer weather before the heatwaves made the outdoors unbearable. No season could be truly predictable in the Midwest.

The catered lunch was a build-your-own-burger setup because Hannah hadn't felt like taking on the challenge of retrieving individual orders from each person in our office. The burgers weren't phenomenal by any means, but burgers were meant to be eaten fresh off the grill. Couldn't complain about free food, after all.

"Want to go to the pool this afternoon?" I asked Ariella on the streetcar ride back to our apartment building. I pushed down the nagging thought of seeing her in a swimsuit.

"I can't because then my hair will be soaked when I put on the wig later," she said, and I felt like an idiot for not thinking of that myself. It's a wonder she could even properly wear a wig over her thick, dark curls, but adding water to the equation would ruin any disguise. When she washed her hair at night, it would still be fairly damp the next morning. She hated using a blow dryer on it because she thought it made her hair frizz more. My hair only took an hour to dry at the most.

I glanced at the weather display on my watch, noting the high temperature today would only be in the low 80s. "We could just go to the game yard and play cornhole instead," I suggested.

"I don't think you know what you're getting into, but challenge accepted." Her smile was as bright as the afternoon sun.

We both stopped by our respective apartments to change into casual clothes before meeting on the rooftop. Although some businesses abided by summer hours and gave employees some, if not all, Friday afternoons off, the game yard was deserted. The pool had a few residents taking advantage of the sunny weather, but Ariella and I would likely be the only ones here for a few hours. Her sunshine yellow shorts complimented the glow of her sun-tanned skin. If I weren't so competitive, I would have been completely distracted by her. It never mattered what she wore, though certain colors seemed to catch my eye more than others.

"Do you think we'll catch Sullivan cheating tonight?" Her question carried a hit of worry in its tone.

"I think it depends on if it was him on the streetcar on Monday," I said because it seemed like the obvious response. "If it was him, I think we shouldn't have any problems getting evidence. Someone who is that careless when their girlfriend is in town will be much more careless while she's away on the east coast. He has to know that you live around here and likely take the streetcar to work regularly."

"I hope you're right." I hope I'm right as well. It was one thing for Ariella to get involved in this situation, but it was another for me to be in on it. Over the years, I had never been sure of Kathleen's opinion of me. On one hand, she could be protective of Ariella; however, sometimes she looked at me as if she was aware of how deep my feelings were for her younger sister. It was likely a mix of both.

She and I were equally matched at this game, drawing a crowd as others gradually ventured to the rooftop. I could hear spectators making bets on which of us would walk away the victor. If I were playing against any girl I was trying to impress, I would have let her win by now, but I didn't need to impress my best friend. When she overshot her throw, I tossed my last bean bag into the hole of the board. She rolled her eyes in mock frustration, but I could tell she was relieved that the competition was finally over.

She followed me back to my apartment, and I pulled out the last bag of microwaveable popcorn in my stash. "Hey, can you add popcorn to your grocery list so that I remember to get some?" I asked her as I punched in the numbers on my microwave.

She opened her phone and said, "You know, you could just make your own list. It's not that difficult to keep a list on your phone in the Notes app. You can even set it to automatically open your list when you're near the grocery store. Technology makes some lazy, but it also removes a lot of excuses that people make." But relying on her for my list gave me an excuse to stick by her side when we go shopping.

I continued her soapbox with some opinions of my own. "Like the people who don't know how Do Not Disturb works. Or that you can set different alarms to go off automatically on varying days of the week if your wakeup time isn't always the same. Technology is at the point that if you're willing to pay, you can control your garage door with your phone as well as lock other doors in the house. Smartphones are highly underutilized for all the things they can do."

"Too bad we can't access Sullivan's location without permission," she said with slight sarcasm. "It would take some of the guesswork out of our mission. That would be an invasion of his privacy though."

I sat down next to her on the sectional. "Stop whining and eat your popcorn. He'll probably stop by your sister's place after work, so we need to make sure we're there by five to be safe, in case he got off work early. I still can't believe you talked me into this." I lobbed a piece of popcorn in the air and caught it with my mouth like I did every time I had a snack that I could catch easily. I didn't have to look at Ariella to know she was shaking her head at me.

"I should have thought this through more," she said as the doubt began to creep into her voice. "I know what car he drives, and he has unique license plate covers, but it's not a small apartment complex. It might take us a while to find his car. We could miss him and not realize it."

"Ariella, it's going to be fine," I said to reassure her. I'd lost count of how many times I'd said those words. "We can even hang out at the entrance to the parking garage and wait for him to drive inside. Or maybe we should be in the lobby close to the elevators so we can see when he leaves. It's up to you." To lighten the mood, I threw a piece of popcorn at her. Unsurprisingly, she caught it with her mouth. Her years of playing softball in high school were proof of her hand-eye coordination.

She seemed lost in thought until she said, “We should stay in the parking garage once we find the SUV. At the small chance that he has another girl with him instead of meeting one somewhere, he wouldn’t bring her inside. The staff know both Sullivan and Kathleen and have seen them together enough to be suspicious about another girl with him.”

I glanced at the clock on the wall and her half-full bowl of popcorn. Subtly, I leaned over to help her finish some of what she had left, but it wasn’t subtle enough. In response to her glare, I said, “At the rate you’re eating, none of the options will be relevant because he’ll have arrived and left.” That’s all it took to get her to share.

With our wigs and sunglasses to hide our identities, we both turned on location sharing on our phones. One Light and Two Light (and soon to be Three Light and Four Light) were in the same neighborhood of the city known as Power and Light. It was annoying because it was clever. It was also convenient because Kathleen’s apartment wasn’t far from ours. I methodically drove around the Two Light parking garage while Ariella kept her eyes peeled for Sullivan’s SUV.

“That’s it!” She pointed to an SUV with leprechauns on the license plate cover. I parked in the nearest spot I could find. “Thanks for driving.”

This whole plan would have been thwarted from the beginning if we had taken her car instead. I said, “Well, I couldn’t let you drive since he would recognize your car.

That aquamarine Prius is great for finding your car in the grocery store parking lot, but horrible for spying. It's too recognizable to be stealthy."

"Not all of us got a practically brand-new Volvo passed down to us by our fathers as a college graduation gift," she said with her attention glued to the SUV. My parents were financially well-off enough that my father bought himself a Tesla and gave me his Volvo.

"Your parents helped you with the down payment for your Prius. They would have helped you buy any reasonably priced hybrid you chose. Gives you one less excuse to visit them if you get good gas economy."

Before she could reply to my rebuttal, we heard a chirp and saw flashing lights coming from Sullivan's SUV. Using my rearview and side mirrors, I stealthily watched as he climbed into his car and started the engine. From the time he drove away toward the exit, I counted fifteen seconds in my head before reversing my car out of the spot. I stayed close enough to keep our eyes on him while still far enough away that he wouldn't suspect he was being followed. We hadn't driven far when he parked in a lot off Baltimore Avenue. Rather than immediately do the same, I drove around the block.

"What if we miss him?" Ariella asked as I continued with the plan we had discussed earlier. I ignored her to avoid a futile argument. When we passed the parking lot again, I could see Sullivan walking on 14th Street toward Main Street. We stopped by a red light at the intersection long enough to watch Sullivan as he crossed two streets and disappeared through the front doors of Blue Sushi.

"How does sushi sound to you?" I asked as I parked in the lot on Truman and Main.

"It would have been cheaper to walk and take the streetcar here," she said about Sullivan's poor planning.

"Maybe he wants his car nearby when he's done," I guessed, "but that doesn't make sense. Two Light is next door to us. Let's go see who he's with before we jump to conclusions about this."

"It'll look weird if we wear our sunglasses inside," she said.

I shrugged and got out of the car. I doubted anyone would pay attention to us. Being out with her like this almost felt like a date, especially when I told the hostess we needed a table for two. The restaurant was busy and only getting busier since it was a Friday night, but we managed to get a table amid the weekend crowd. I could tell Ariella was anxious. I had a plan though.

After ordering our entrees, I stood up and said, "I'm going to the restroom if I can even find it in this madness."

Going to the restroom was a valid excuse as any to wander around and track down Sullivan. The man in question was at a table on the way to the restrooms, making this mission easier than I had anticipated. Sitting next to him was the girl I recognized from the streetcar. Keeping a steady walking pace, I pulled out my phone as if I were checking something. Instead, I took several photos of Sullivan as he kissed his date. Running on adrenaline, I quickly used the restroom before returning to mine and Ariella's table.

"I got it," I smiled with excitement.

"How?" It was well worth it to see the way her face lit up.

"I saw him on the way to the restrooms," I said. "I really did need to go, but I also knew it would give me the perfect excuse to walk through other parts of the restaurant. He's sitting at a table with the same girl I saw him with on the streetcar. He was so oblivious that I got photos of their kissing without his noticing someone was watching." I swiped through the evidence on my camera roll.

"Too bad we already ordered," she said and leaned back in her chair. This girl needed to have a greater appreciation for good food.

I said, "Too bad? This was as good an excuse as any to get sushi."

The white tuna sashimi was well worth the spy mission. I requested chopsticks for our table for the sake of an "authentic experience." Even Ariella's shrimp tempura maki looked delicious, but I knew she would eat it all without my help.

I insisted on paying for both our meals but didn't argue with her when she contributed to the tip. The streets and sidewalks were bustling with people, bikes, scooters, and cars as the warmth of the summer day began to fade. We joined the group of people waiting at the pedestrian crosswalk. I stiffened at the sound of Sullivan's loud voice as it grew closer to us. I could sense the panic radiating from Ariella as my mind clung to the only plan that seemed to make sense.

Before I could change my mind or overthink it, I pulled her close and kissed her. It was less about trying to hide our faces from Sullivan and more about doing the very thing I'd imagined for years. My heart raced as I kissed the girl I'd always thought I'd end up with in the end, and she kissed me back as if she felt the same.

"Get a room!" Sullivan said as he walked past us.

Remembering that we were standing on the sidewalk of Main Street on a Friday night, I stopped the kiss, resting my forehead against hers as we caught our breath and waited for the pedestrian crossing light to change again. When the walk symbol appeared, we distanced ourselves and walked back to my car without eye contact or speaking. As soon as we were inside the car, we both removed our wigs, and I drove us back to our nearby apartment building.

Neither of us said anything, but I knew we both needed time to process the dynamic shift in our relationship that I had perpetuated. Dating Ariella could never be casual; it would be intentional steps toward marriage and the rest of our lives together. I was sure it was what I wanted, but I couldn't be sure it was what she wanted.

I sent Ariella all the photos of Sullivan that I had taken at the restaurant and texted her about what time we should meet for grocery shopping. The kiss was too serious of a topic to discuss over text. It would have to be in person.

AUTHOR'S SHAMELESS PLUG

I've heard other authors refer to cities as living organisms that grow and evolve, and it might be one of the most accurate examples I've heard to describe it. Change is a bittersweet balance of both exciting and heartbreaking. After living over a decade of my life in the Kansas City metro area, I can definitively say that many things have changed for the better since I moved here as an eighteen-year-old college freshman. The streetcar didn't exist when I was a student, and the north and south extensions are currently under construction as I'm drafting and editing. Soon, students from my alma mater at the University of Missouri-Kansas City will be able to walk to the streetcar and take public transportation to many different neighborhoods in the heart of the city.

Between drafts of this story, the restaurant where Kendrick and Ariella catch Sullivan closed and another sushi restaurant opened in the same location. While doing self-editing, I changed the name to that of the new restaurant. If a coworker hadn't talked about it at work, I may not have even known about that change until after publishing this book. Cities like Kansas City are in constant states of change. This story is just a snippet in a set place and time. Ten years from now, many details of this book might no longer exist, and that's something we need to keep in mind as readers and authors. As long as you don't use my book as your tour guide when you come to visit, you won't be disappointed or lost.

With that in mind, I'll leave you with a few suggestions. If you have any interest in American football, you should go to at least one Chiefs game in Arrowhead Stadium. There's a reason it holds the world record for the loudest outdoor stadium. There's also a reason the stadium has been around for over 50 years. In a few years, it'll be one of the venues used for hosting the 2026 FIFA World Cup. I also suggest visiting Union Station and Liberty Memorial. If you have any interest in history, go to the World War I Museum. The Nelson-Atkinson Museum of Art is also well worth the visit. I could go on forever, so maybe you should just do some research because I'm still discovering new things about this metro. Kansas City is one of those up-and-coming destinations, and I'm glad it's where I've spent my twenties.

I somehow managed to write a story mostly set in Kansas City without mentioning jazz, fountains, or any of the famous BBQ restaurants. Maybe next time.

Acknowledgments

I drafted this book in 2020. Yes, **that** 2020. Until October of that year, the only story idea I had was a dystopian love story taking place in the midst of a pandemic, for obvious reasons. I had been working from home for seven months, which meant having extra time to write 50,000 words during National Novel Writing Month (NaNoWriMo) in November. This is the first of my NaNoWriMo drafts finally making it to publication.

I don't remember how I stumbled across the myth of kissing the Blarney Stone, but I knew it would make for a good story. As of the publication of this book, I've never been to Ireland. I watched several videos and did a virtual tour of Blarney Castle. It was 2020, so traveling wasn't an option. Using my own city as the setting for the remainder of the story wasn't as easy as I'd anticipated. And, of course, I had to include a piece of Italy there at the end.

Editing this story was also much harder than I'd anticipated. Not only did I continually procrastinate on when I would start editing (I should have known that I wouldn't get any editing done while in Europe), but when I did finally dig in, it was while processing a lot of unexpected emotions. Instead of finishing in April and May, it became July and August.

Ally and Erica, I wouldn't have been able to get this ready for the general public without your extensive and specific feedback. Patrick and Britni, thank you for being willing to read through the early draft. To all my friends in our growing writing group, thanks for the encouragement to keep pushing through. That also goes for the people who have been asking for another book.

My first book took around six years from the first draft to the final. This one is only three years, so it's an improvement when it comes to turnaround time. Maybe one of these days I'll get something out within a year of the first draft.

ABRIDGED AUTOBIOGRAPHY

As a second-generation American, I share a love for both my country and for all the places abroad that I haven't seen yet or that I want to see again. It doesn't help that I have enough nationalities mixed into my genetics that I have yet to see all the places my ancestors are from.

I love to read and write almost as much as I love all things Italian–the food, the language, the country, the leather, the coffee, the food, and the list goes on. The slight obsession with Italy is evident in my stories. My preferred schedule is that of a night owl, though I'm adaptable when necessary as long as I have caffeine. When I'm not lost in another world or country, Kansas City is home and the Chiefs are my NFL team.

Jesus is an essential part of my life and identity and a big reason why I keep on writing happy endings. Sometimes I write as a way to balance the power between my imagination and the logical part of my brain, the side that tries to remain tethered to reality.

lbethcampbell.com

But really, the best place for updates on future releases is Instagram

@L.BethCampbell

ALSO BY L. BETH CAMPBELL

The Arranged Crown

Printed in the USA
CPSIA information can be obtained
at www.ICGtesting.com
LVHW031353230923
759051LV00019B/61/J

9 781960 639073